CAUGHT BETWEEN
TWO
WORLDS

BY

G.S. WILLMOTT

CONTENTS

LIFE IS GOOD

CHAPTER 1

Melbourne University

November 1965

Ross Hargraves was finishing his economics paper. It was his last exam. All going well, he would graduate with a degree in Business Studies, majoring in accounting. He was due to meet his mates at the Corkman Irish Pub at 5 pm to celebrate the end of university days and the beginning of a new life earning money and spending most of it on wine, women and song.

Ross arrived at the pub thirty minutes late; he had to do a few things on the way. The saloon bar was full of students, mostly drinking Guinness. Even the girls were knocking back the dark amber liquid. Ross anticipated a good night and he wasn't disappointed.

'Hey Rossco, over here mate!' yelled his best mate Ian "Oogie" Jones.

'G' day Oogie.'

'What are you drinking, mate?' asked Oogie.

'Just the usual.'

'Right, one Guinness coming up.'

Ian returned from the bar with a pint of the Irish brew. 'Get that down, mate. We have some serious drinking and, with luck, rooting tonight.'

'That all sounds good to me.'

'Getting off the drinking and rooting for a wee while... How do you think you went in the final exams?' asked Oogie.

'I'm quietly confident; economics may prove to be my downfall but I don't think so. How about you?'

'I reckon I pissed it in.'

'I'm not surprised. You will probably dux the Engineering School.'

'Maybe, but I wouldn't bet on it. There's plenty of smart cookies out there.'

'Hey, Oogie, have you thought about getting a job yet?'

'Yeah, I had one of the big civil engineering firms approach me.'

'Are you going to take it?'

'I'm not sure. What's worrying me is conscription and the fucking Vietnam War. If my number comes up it's all superfluous.'

'Yeah, I suppose I'm in the same boat,' said Ross.

'If our birthdates get picked in the ballot, it's goodbye job, goodbye money and goodbye plenty of sex,' said Oogie.

'Hello khaki, hot humid jungle and people we don't know trying to kill us,' said Ross.

The Birthday Ballot

'Okay, that's enough of that. We have to charm some fillies with the express purpose of taking them home for some serious hanky panky,' said Oogie.

'Excellent suggestion; do you see any contenders?'

'As a matter of fact, I do. Do you see those two girls at the end of the bar?'

'You mean the blonde and the redhead with the big tits.'

'That's exactly who I mean.'

'Which one do you fancy?' asked Ross.

'Seeing I spotted them I'll go for the redhead.'

'I thought you might. The blonde suits me fine.'

The two good-looking boys sauntered up to their prey and introduced themselves.

A conversation began. The young women had just completed three years at teacher's college and were looking forward to a two week holiday at Surfers Paradise in Queensland. After several margaritas, Lorreta and Kate were feeling quite tipsy.

'Girls, Ross and I rent a terrace house very close by. Would you care to come back for a coffee and port?'

'Both girls knew what they really meant was, "Would you care to come back to our house and get thoroughly fucked."

'Yes, that sounds wonderful, boys.'

'Excellent, it's only a five-minute walk. Shall we go?' xxx

Once they reached the terrace coffee and port was forgotten. Oogie and Jane headed upstairs to his bedroom. Ross and Loretta didn't even make it that far. The sofa in the living room sufficed.

Jane and Loretta rang for a taxi at 2 am. They flew to Queensland the next day.

The Terrace House

Melbourne January 1966

Oogie and Ross decided they would listen to the ballot results at the pub. They both figured they could get pissed if their birthdays came up. It was also decided they would get pissed if they missed out.

Ian was born on the 15th of February.

5

Ross was born on the 20th of March.

The barmaid, Sally, turned on the radio and tuned it to the ABC where the broadcast was due to begin in five minutes.

At least thirty young men listened eagerly to the dulcet tones of the ABC announcer introducing the ballot.

The 15th of February was called. Ian was going in.

The 20th of March was not called.

It was easy to determine which among the 20-year-olds had been called up and which had dodged a bullet. It was a strange night at the pub and most went home early.

The next day, Oogie telephoned his mother and father, Malcolm and Jess, and arranged to go home for dinner the following night.

Ross did the same although the atmosphere at the Hargraves household was one of elation rather than trepidation.

April 1

Victoria Barracks Melbourne

Having passed his medical examinations, Oogie was formally accepted into the Australian Army. He was now required to board a bus bound for the army training camp at Puckapunyal.

He sat next to a bloke with red hair and freckles, who hardly looked old enough to be conscripted. His name was Simon Cameron and he said he grew up in Ballarat.

The two young men became great friends until they were separated in Vietnam.

The bus arrived at camp at 9 pm. The conscripts were ordered to leave the bus and form up into a line, two by two. The Sergeant in charge ordered the young conscripts to march to the barracks. Forty men were assigned to each hut. The Sergeant instructed the men to keep the barracks neat and tidy at all times. If a particular bed were not made correctly, the whole hut would pay the penalty.

Once the Sergeant had departed, the men could talk among themselves.

'Fucking hell, this is going to be a barrel of laughs, mate,' said Simon to Oogie.

'It's straight out of the movies; I can't wait for marching training tomorrow. It will probably follow on from "how to clean your boots properly".'

'Yeah, I think we'd better get some sleep. Tomorrow could be a long day.'

'I reckon you could be right. Goodnight, mate.'

Reveille sounded at 6 am. The men were required to assemble in front of the barracks by 6.30 am. They ran for four kilometers, then showered and dressed in their new uniforms. Breakfast followed and then a day of training took place.

Oogie was right; they were trained on how to march and how to take care of their equipment, including their boots.

Oogie and Simon spent 10 weeks together at the Puckapunyal base, training to be soldiers.

Simon described the training in a letter to his parents like this:

"We were quickly introduced to the discipline of army life and it seemed that orders were coming from all directions".

"Quick march, left right left, lift those arms up, about-face and halt," was the norm.

"We were taught how to march, listen, and obey commands. We went on early morning runs and underwent a fitness regime to gain the stamina needed for war. We also learned to fight, defend the cause and kill the enemy if required."

It was a 10-week boot camp, with no leave for the first six weeks.

"We shot rifles and machine guns, threw hand grenades and learned to fight with bayonets fixed. Keep the letters coming, Mum and Dad."

It was a world of polished boots, badges, and belt buckles, along with army greens, berets and slouch hats.

One of the toughest things to bear was getting their hair cut. Both Oogie and Simon had beautiful long wavy hair; Simon's was auburn and Oogie's was blond. They were both popular with the girls. Now they were hardly distinguishable from all the other short back and side soldiers.

Their diet also changed now they were eating in an army mess hall. Cooked meals from Mum were missed. In the field, army ration packs were their source of nourishment.

All the men were given lectures on the enemy, shown documentaries on discipline, and taught how to react to an ambush.

At the end of the ten-week training camp, some of the soldiers were ordered back to barracks for reassignment. The balance would be heading for Vietnam. Oogie and Simon fell into the latter group.

'Well, mate, it's off to Vietnam we go. What do you reckon about that?'

'To be honest, Oogie, after all that training I'm rather pleased to be going. At least we'll be able to use our newfound skills.'

'Yeah, like how to shoot some little Vietnamese soldier.'

'Don't be sarcastic, mate. We've got a fucking job to do and by crikey, I'm going to do my best to complete it.'

'Okay, okay, don't get all shirty with me. I was just joking. I'm with you 100%.'

July 1 1966

Several army trucks pulled up inside the parade ground at Puckapunyal. Fewer than two hundred conscripts joined the convoy and were transported to the RAAF Williams Airbase at Laverton.

A RAAF Boeing 707 was waiting on the tarmac. The only civilians joining them would be the pilots and the flight attendants. The boys would be served tea or coffee and a light, almost edible, meal.

'This is all right, mate. I've never been on a big plane before,' said Oogie.

'Mate, I've never been on any type of plane before. This is a whole new experience.'

'I think this is the easiest it will get for a while.'

'I think you're right, Oogie.'

The flight would take ten hours. Business Class was not an option.

After a very bumpy flight, they landed in Saigon. It was just after midnight, yet the activity at the airport was frenetic. Fighter jets were taking off while others were landing.

'I've never had a sauna but I reckon this fucking humidity and heat would be pretty close,' said Oogie.

'Fucking hell, it is hot and it's the middle of the night. God help us patrolling in the jungle in the middle of the day with a full pack.'

'Welcome to Vietnam.'

Oogie and Simon and the rest of the Battalion were loaded onto American buses.

'Hey, Simon, have you got any idea why these buses are covered in steel mesh?' asked Oogie.

'I wouldn't have a clue, mate. Let's ask the driver. He's an American soldier, so he ought to know.'

'Excuse me, can you tell me why the bus is covered in steel mesh?'

'Yeah, sure. It's there to protect us from hand grenades.'

'Oh, I see. How thoughtful.'

'Welcome to fucking Vietnam, brother,' said Oogie.

The convoy of buses arrived at their destination on the other side of the airfield. Waiting for them were several Caribou military aircraft. The flight to Nui Dat would take an hour. They all hoped they would catch up on some sleep when they arrived.

All the soldiers had a sense of foreboding as they marched across the wet tarmac.

Caribou Transport Plane

Oogie and Simon on the tarmac at Nui Dat

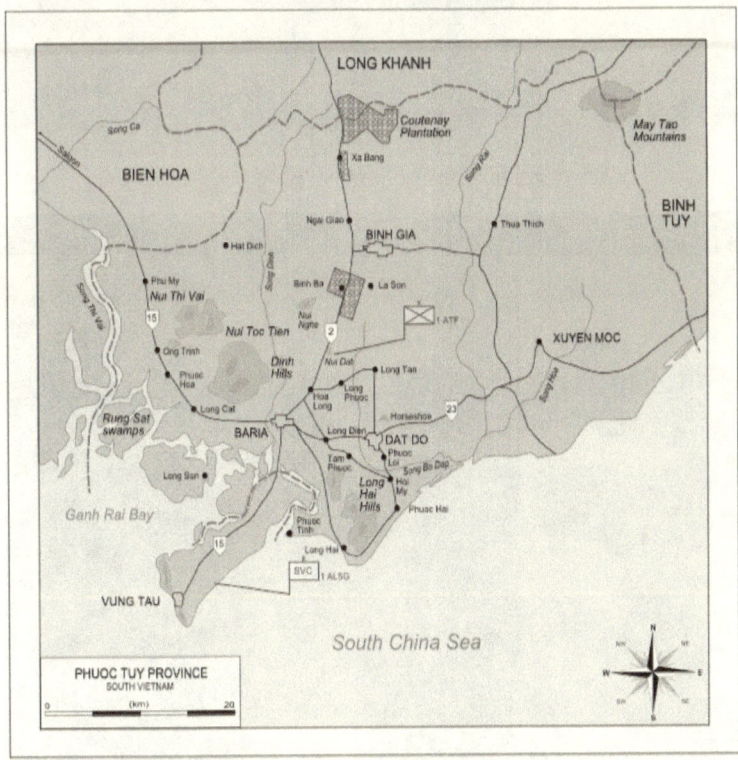

Phuc Tuy Region - Nui Dat AIF Base

Simon and Oogie would get to know the Phuc Tuy region like the back of their hands over the coming twelve months.

The Australian troops were given instructions to erect tents for their interim accommodation.

The first week at Nui Dat base was spent erecting tents and clearing access roads. Time was also spent constructing levies to contain the monsoon water flooding the camp.

Oogie & Simon constructing Levy Bank

Oogie and Simon's Palace

A more sophisticated base was constructed

Nui Dat Base Camp

The boys had hardly settled in when they were ordered to go out on patrol.

Sergeant Phillips entered the newly constructed barracks of the Australian conscripts.

'Men, today you will embark on your first patrol. Have no doubt it will be dangerous. You will be entering enemy territory. The Viet Kong will engage us if they see fit. Look out for your mates at all times.

'Our helicopters will pick us up in one hour. Use the time to check your equipment thoroughly.'

'Can you tell us where we are heading, Sarge?'

'No, I can't. It's classified.'

The twenty-eight men in the platoon checked their LTA1 self-loading rifles and the grenades in their top pockets. Then they heard the distant noise of the helicopters approaching.

'This is it, Simon, it's off to war we go. Good luck, mate. Don't get yourself killed, or I'll have no one to beat at chess.'

Simon laughed. 'I wouldn't be so inconsiderate.'

The platoon boarded the four Huey helicopters and headed for their unknown destination. Flying over the terrain gave the soldiers an idea of what they were about to face.

The helicopters landed just outside the village of Hoa Long. There had been some enemy activity reported in and around the village. It was the patrol's task to cleanse the village of the enemy.

Once the soldiers alighted, the four helicopters headed back to Nui Dat and relative safety.

Lieutenant Humphries led the patrol. Sergeant Phillips was his deputy.

The Lieutenant indicated to the men to follow him into the village. If there were any Viet Cong, they would have disappeared when they heard the helicopters. The usual tactic was to hide outside the village until the Australians entered the area. They would then return and attack.

Oogie whispered to his mate Simon, 'Not much going on, mate; we might be lucky this time.'

'I wouldn't count on it. These bastards are meant to be tricky.'

'Yeah, I suppose you're right. Back me up entering this hut. It could be booby-trapped.'

'Remember what the Sergeant said. Push the door open with your foot.'

'Are you ready?'

'Let's go.'

Ian Oogie Jones kicked the door as hard as he could and jumped back. His suspicions were correct— the door had been booby-trapped.

Booby-Trapped Door

If he hadn't been cautious he would have been killed. The fact the booby-trap had been set proved the Viet Kong controlled this village.

The Lieutenant ordered the platoon to search the entire village, being ever aware of more booby-traps. They discovered only women and children and old men. The Viet Kong were long gone.

The Sergeant radioed for the helicopters to pick up the platoon and take them back to Nui Dat.

AUSTRALIAN WAR MEMORIAL   EKN C7 0 3C VN

'Don't you love the sound of a helicopter?' asked Oogie.

'Yeah, I do if it's taking us back to base. I don't like it when they are dropping us off into a potential firefight,' said Simon.

It took fifteen minutes to fly back to base camp at Nui Dat. The platoon had time to swallow a can of cold beer before they hit the mess tent for some cordon bleu cuisine.

Preparing a meal from the can

Each day, Oogie, Simon, and their platoon would patrol the areas close to their base. They did come across enemy fire regularly. A bullet in his left eye killed one of the men in their platoon. Simon was behind him and he couldn't believe it. There was no scream; he just fell to the ground. The platoon let go with a barrage of automatic fire, killing six of the enemy.

THE BATTLE OF LONG TAN

CHAPTER 2

August 18 1966

The Battle of Long Tan

The Battle of Long Tan became a life-changing event for Oogie Jones. The battle took place in a rubber plantation in South Vietnam in 1966. The odds were well and truly against Oogie's platoon and their brothers in arms. It could have been an Australian military disaster but is instead remembered as a decisive victory.

August 17 1966, Nui Dat

Oogie was sound asleep in the tent he shared with Simon and four other diggers. Out of the jungle surrounding the camp came a barrage of mortars. Quickly, the soldiers grabbed their guns. Trousers were an optional extra.

The Australians began to return fire. The fight was over in fifteen minutes, and fortunately none of the Australians was hit.

While the attack caused only minimal damage, it concerned the Australian Task Force Commander, Brigadier Oliver Jackson. He recognised the base's potential for a significant VC attack. Something had to be done.

August 18, 1966

D Company 6 RAR Battalion, consisting of 105 Australians, along with a three-man New Zealand artillery team, entered the Long Tan rubber plantations searching for the VC who attacked the previous night.

About 3.30pm, a group of Viet Cong stumbled into the middle of the patrolling Australian soldiers. The diggers opened fire, wounding one and forcing the others to flee deep into the plantation.

The Australian soldiers continued their advance, the three platoons of D Company - designated 10, 11 and 12 - taking up positions around the rubber plantation.

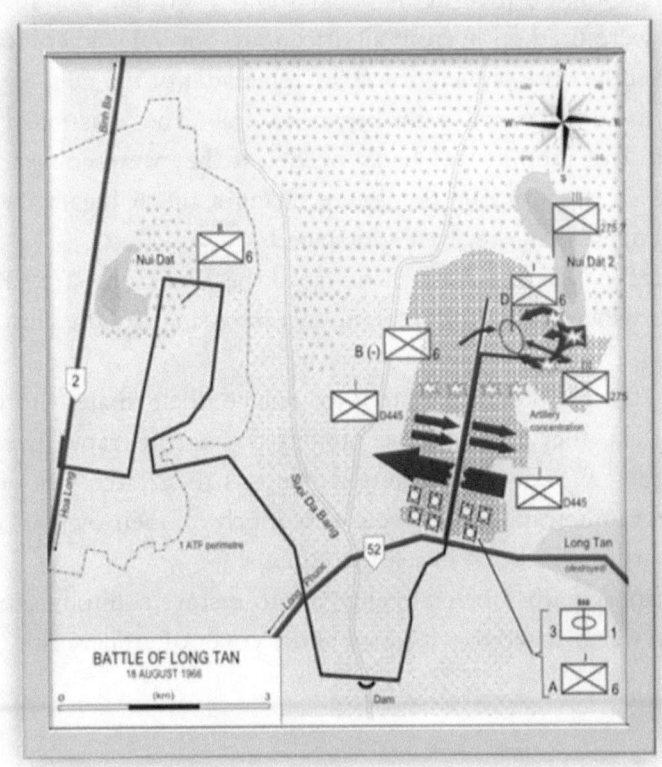

BATTLE OF LONG TAN
18 AUGUST 1966

The 11th platoon, 28 men in all, walked into a VC ambush around 4.00 pm. They were fired upon from all directions. Several soldiers were killed and the relentless fire pinned down the remainder of the men.

The usual torrential rain began to fall. The Australian officers realised artillery support was badly needed if they were going to survive this battle. It was obvious they were facing a much bigger and better-equipped enemy than they first anticipated.

The reality was the Australians faced the Viet Cong 275th Regiment and the Provincial Mobile Battalion, encompassing 2,500 enemy soldiers in total.

The 10th platoon attempted to relieve their mates in the 11th. Unfortunately, they too became pinned down with rapid fire coming from all sides. What made matters worse was their radio was destroyed. Without communication, they were very much on their own. They could not direct artillery or bring in reinforcements.

A radio operator braved enemy fire to restore communications and 10 Platoon was ordered to withdraw under cover of artillery fire.

While the battle was taking place, Oogie and Simon were napping in their tent, having been out on patrol for most of the previous night hunting the VC who attacked the base.

Captain Gilmore woke them, ordering both soldiers to help load ammo boxes into the helicopters.

Oogie and Simon then boarded the chopper with the purpose of dropping the boxes down to the besieged Australian soldiers.

The helicopters found platoon 11 and the six diggers including Oogie and Simon were grateful they were not joining their brothers in arms on that fateful day.

As the helicopter rose and began to turn for the base, a barrage of automatic fire killed both pilots. The chopper plummeted to the ground. All but Oogie were killed on impact.

Oogie looked around the interior of the helicopter. It was obvious all had been killed, including his good mate Simon.

He felt an intense pain in his left leg and when he looked down, he saw his femur protruding through his skin.

'Well, I hope that's not completely fucked. I want to play football again,' he muttered.

He lay there in pain for what seemed like hours. He'd have thought his comrades would have rescued him by now.

At last, he heard voices, but it wasn't what he had hoped to hear. A Viet Cong soldier leaned into the cabin. He perused the carnage and then noticed Oogie.

'Bạn có thấy người sống sót nào không?' 'Do you see any survivors?' asked the platoon leader, Chi.

'Dường như chỉ có một. Phần còn lại đã chết,' answered Thao.

'There seems to be one only. The rest are dead.'

'Tôi có nên đặt một viên đạn vào đầu anh ta?' 'Should I put a bullet in his head?'

'Không, chúng tôi cần thẩm vấn anh ta ở căn cứ.' 'No, we need to interrogate him back at the base.'

'Kéo anh ta ra khỏi chiếc chopper để chúng tôi có thể thấy mức độ thương tích của anh ta. Nếu chúng quá tệ, một viên đạn vào đầu sẽ là một lựa chọn tốt.' 'Pull him out of the chopper so we can see the extent of his injuries. If they are too bad, a bullet in the head would be a good option.'

The Viet Cong soldiers decided a broken leg was not too serious. They decided to take him back to base camp several kilometres away deep in the jungle.

Melbourne August 18 1966

Oogie's father, John, was a doctor; a cardiologist. He had just completed heart surgery on a sixty-year-old man. His wife, Anna, had arranged for them to join their good friends the Bakers for dinner at Florentinos. Although tired, he was looking forward to it. Anna picked him up from Prince Henry's Hospital. The restaurant was only a short distance away in Bourke Street.

John leaned across and kissed his wife.

'How did the operation go, darling?'

'It was pretty straight forward, no complications.'

'You must be feeling tired. Are you okay?'

'Yeah, I'm okay. I'm looking forward to seeing the Bakers. We haven't caught up with them for ages.'

Anna was a very careful driver; too careful in John's opinion.

As the car was crossing Melbourne's busiest intersection, Flinders and Swanston Streets, a car being chased by the police slammed into them. John and Anna were killed instantly.

Oogie would not know what had happened for many years.

Meanwhile, the battle continued. Vietnamese forces advanced on 11 Platoon in a bid to negate the artillery support.

Artillery was moved closer to the pinned down troops, with shells falling less than 100 metres from the Australians. Friendly fire casualties were inevitable.

Boys in War

A resupplied 11 Platoon moved to withdraw, meeting up with parts of 12 Platoon who were engaged nearby and eventually reformed with the rest of D Company.

The Australian forces were deployed in a defensive position as the enemy closed in, launching human wave assaults of infantry across the rubber plantation. Wave after wave of black-uniformed seasoned soldiers just kept coming despite the Australian artillery taking a terrible toll on their numbers.

After several hours of intense fighting, reinforcements from B Company arrived on foot, along with A Company on board armoured personnel carriers dispatched from Nui Dat.

Three-and-a-half hours after the battle had started, the Vietnamese disengaged and the fighting stopped as quickly as it had begun.

Over the next two days, clean-up operations were carried out on the battlefield, rescuing the wounded and recovering the bodies of those killed.

Eighteen Australians were killed plus the five in the helicopter. Twenty-one were wounded. The whereabouts of private Ian Jones remained a mystery.

Two hundred and forty-five Vietnamese dead were found on the battlefield, with captured documents later suggesting hundreds more had been killed or wounded.

The Australian soldiers had been outnumbered 20 to 1 and despite their success against overwhelming odds, the Battle of Long Tan was still the costliest battle for Australia during the entire Vietnam War.

So This Is Hell

Chapter 3

The leader of the Viet Cong 275 Regiment, Chi instructed two of his men to bathe Oogie's wound with an antiseptic made from tree roots. They then bandaged the leg and fashioned a crutch from a tree branch. This was not done as an act of kindness. Chi wanted his prisoner to make it back to base camp alive so that he could be interrogated.

Oogie had no delusions; he knew he would be tortured until he divulged all that he knew. The truth was he knew fuck all. He was a foot soldier; a national service lackey. What in the fuck could he tell these bastards?

Oogie found it very tough going through the jungle, but each time he stopped to rest he was pushed forward. After two very difficult days, the group arrived at their jungle base camp.

The camp was partly above ground and partly comprised of tunnels. Oogie was placed in what effectively was a bamboo cage.

Oogie knew life was not going to be easy from then on. The cage offered no shelter and the monsoonal rains drenched him every day. Being damp was nothing compared to what the VC had in store for their prisoner. After the first week, they changed the regime. At night, he was tied spreadeagled on the ground to four stakes. This not only prohibited him from escaping; it also prohibited him from getting any sleep. In the mornings, his face would be so swollen from mosquito bites he was unable to see clearly.

His captors did let him walk in the jungle escorted every now and again.

On one of these walks he took the opportunity to escape into the jungle but it was a short-lived freedom; he was recaptured and subjected to a range of tortures.

Oogie knew he was in trouble when his captors hung him upside down over a fire ants' nest. These ferocious ants covered Oogie's face until eventually he lost consciousness.

At night, they suspended him in a freezing well. He knew if he fell asleep he would drown.

Other times, he was dragged by water buffalo through villages, his guards laughing as they goaded both him and the animal with a whip.

Bloodied and almost broken, he was asked by Viet Cong officers to sign a document condemning Australia and America. He refused, so the torture intensified. Tiny wedges of bamboo were inserted under his fingernails and into incisions on his body to grow and fester.

Oogie was eventually brought to a prison camp near the village of Par Kung where he met several other POWs. Chi remained the camp commandant. The fact Chi could speak English made it a little easier for the American POWs to make requests such as bandages etc.

They were:

Pisidhi Indradat (Thai)

Prasit Promsuwan (Thai)

Prasit Thanee (Thai)

Y.C. To (Chinese)

Duane W. Martin (American)

Eugene DeBruin (American)

Apart from Martin, an air force helicopter pilot who had been shot down in North Vietnam nearly a year before, the other prisoners were civilians employed by Air America, a civilian airline owned by the Central Intelligence Agency. Oogiee hoped there would be strength in numbers; maybe together they could all escape.

When he met the other POWs he was horrified. There was one man carrying his intestines cupped in his hands. Another had barely any teeth left; the few he had were badly ulcerated and extremely painful. He begged the other POWs to knock them out with a rock.

All the prisoners were in very bad shape. Oogie knew he had to escape or he would end up like these poor fellows inside six months. He informed the other prisoners of his intention to escape on his first day in the camp. They all suggested he wait until the monsoon season arrived, ensuring he would always have access to fresh water.

A few weeks after Oogie had arrived in the camp, the Viet Cong moved them all to another camp just twenty kilometres away at Hoi Het.

There was a division among the POWs; those who wanted to escape, including Oogie, Martin and Prasit, and the others who were opposed.

The food made available to them became less and less until the daily ration consisted of a cup of rice to be shared by all of them. The POWs occasionally caught a snake or a rat, which would be devoured by the prisoners; it was the only meat they could get.

Sleeping at night was difficult; the men were shackled together with their feet locked in foot blocks. They couldn't move, and together with the chronic dysentery most of them suffered they were forced to lie in their own excrement until being released in the morning.

Prasit Promsuwan, a Thai prisoner, overheard two guards discussing a plan to take the prisoners into the jungle and shoot them all. They were planning to make it look like an escape attempt. Then they could return home to their villages.

Prasit informed the other POWs as to what he had heard. Oogie was determined that he and the other men should escape as soon as possible. They lay bound in their shackles that night and devised a plan.

At lunchtime, the guards would lay down their weapons; this and the evening meal were the only times the guards were not armed. They agreed midday would be the best time to enact the plan as they could see their way when they entered the jungle.

Oogie and another prisoner loosened the floorboards, enabling them to squeeze through. The plan was to rush the guards, seize their weapons, and disappear into the jungle.

The Escape

October 26 1966

The group managed to break out of their manacles using sharpened bamboo to pick the locks. The same method was used to free their feet. They all squeezed out between the floorboards and lay in wait for the guards to begin their lunch of rice and deer. They made their move. Running about five metres, the prisoners grabbed the weapons, including a M1 rifle, Chinese automatic rifles, and a sub machine gun. Oogie grabbed a AK47 just as five of the guards rushed him. He managed to shoot and kill three. The other two escaped into the jungle.

The seven prisoners split into three groups.

DeBruin was originally supposed to go with Oogie and Martin, but he decided to be with To, supporting his Chinese friend who was recovering from a fever and would be unable to keep up. They intended to get over the nearest ridge and wait for rescue.

Oogie and Duane Martin decided to head for the Mekong River, enabling them to escape to Thailand.

At last the two men were free; one Australian; the other American. They no longer had to endure the horrors of the VC camp, but escape brought its own torments.

Soon, the two men's feet were white and mangled from trekking through the dense jungle. This was similar to what the soldiers in the trenches during World War One called "trench feet".

They found the sole of an old tennis shoe, which they took turns wearing, strapping it onto a foot with rattan for a few hours of respite.

They were able to make their way to a fast-flowing river.

Oogie knew this river would lead them to the Mekong.

We knew it would flow into the Mekong River, which would take us over the border into Thailand and safety, thought Oogie.

The men built a raft from logs tied together with rattan and floated downstream, encountering ferocious rapids along the way. At night, they would tie the raft to a solid tree on the riverbank, ensuring the raft wasn't swept away by the fast flowing torrent. The men would wake to be greeted by hundreds of leeches sucking their much-needed blood.

Oogie observed villages which looked familiar. He was sure they had passed them days before; they had been going around in a circle. It became obvious this river would not take them to the Mekong and freedom.

They set up camp in an abandoned village where they found shelter from the incessant rain. Although Oogie and Duane had brought rice with them and were able to find other food, they were still on the verge of starvation.

The two escapees were hoping to send a signal to an American C-130 which they had seen crossing over the village on a regular basis. Using the gunpowder from some carbine cartridges that they had kept dry they were able to light a fire. They created torches from bamboo and bracken, and waved them when the C-130 flew above the village. To their delight, the plane circled and dropped a couple of flares. They went to sleep that night feeling confident that a rescue mission would free them next morning. No such rescue happened.

When, next morning, they realised there would be no rescue both Oogie and Duane felt totally demoralised.

Duane persuaded Oogie it was worth the risk to approach a nearby village, to see if they could obtain some food. Oogie was reluctant but he would not abandon his friend, so he agreed to go.

They entered the village and saw a young boy playing stick with his dog. The two men approached him smiling and holding out their hands. The boy turned and ran back to his home yelling 'AMERICAN'. A male villager appeared almost immediately and Oogie and Duane kneeled down in supplication. The man swung a machete he was holding, hitting Duane in the leg. He struck again and Duane was decapitated.

Oogie quickly rose to his feet and rushed towards the villager who turned and ran back into the village, losing his rubber thongs in his mad rush to get help. Oogie picked up the thongs and ran back into the jungle before the other villagers confronted him.

The only highlight of his time in the jungle was befriending a bear. It became his substitute dog, following him wherever he went. It helped Oogie to keep his sanity.

He was alone, starving and floating in and out of a hallucinatory state. He had little confidence that he would ever be rescued, but he never gave up trying.

Oogie managed to evade the villagers who were searching for him, by escaping back into the jungle. He returned to the abandoned village that night. When a C-130 came over, Oogie set fire to the huts and burned the village down. The C-130 crew spotted the fires and dropped flares, but even though the crew reported their sighting when they returned to their base at Ubon, Thailand, the fires were not recognised by Intelligence as having been a signal.

The young Australian conscript was at the end of his tether. He had little energy and little hope of being rescued. He stumbled upon a paddy field in a large clearing in the jungle, where he lay down beside the still water, not expecting to wake.

His fate was determined when he was woken by a pretty Vietnamese woman probably about the same age as himself. She could see how badly he had been injured. Her name was Hanh, and she lived in a village nearby. The name of the village was Cao Lanh, and it was located on the left bank of the Mekong River.

When Oogie recovered, he would realise the irony of where he was now located. He had been searching for the Mekong River since his escape without success.

Hanh thought if she brought the man into the village, the elders would kill him. They could not afford to nurture a wounded soldier back to health. The village had barely enough to feed themselves. The rice they grew was mostly traded for other essential commodities.

Hanh knew she needed to bring the soldier back to health by feeding him and dressing his wounds. The first thing she did was carve out a clearing in the jungle where Oogie could lie out of sight from the other villagers. Hanh stole a rug and a blanket from her parents' hut to make him more comfortable. Oogie had access to clean water, which was replenished by Hanh each day. She also fed him rice and pork or chicken twice daily.

Gradually, over a period of weeks, the young Australian gathered strength. He was still far from healthy but he could now walk around, albeit limited by the thick jungle.

Hanh began teaching Oogie Vietnamese. When she brought him his meals, she would point and say the Vietnamese name for the food.

He, in turn, would point and say the English word for the dish. This way they began to communicate in rudimentary Vietnamese and English.

Hanh brought Oogie a bowl of Pho. He asked her what was in it.

'Nước dùng mặn, mì gạo tươi, rắc rau thơm và thịt gà hoặc thịt bò.'

The young woman pointed at the ingredients of the dish. Oogie translated these to beef, noodles, rice and herbs.

After two months had passed, Hanh knew it was time to either say goodbye to Oogie or introduce him to the village with the hope they would accept him.

She attempted to explain the two options to the Australian using English and sign language plus some gestures.

Oogie understood; his preference was to risk going to the village rather than going back to war.

THE VILLAGE PEOPLE

CHAPTER 4

Hanh explained the situation to her mother and father. At first, they were very reluctant to accept an Australian soldier into the fold. After some discussion and a little pleading, they agreed to take Oogie in on a one-month trial basis. The remainder of the villagers would have to accept their decision. Hanh's little brother Binh was quite excited as he welcomed another male in the house. He hoped this man played football (soccer). Binh was eight years younger than his sister; what they call an afterthought.

Cao Lanh consisted of 100 people. It was quite small compared to other villages close by.

Hahn's father, Danh, called a village meeting. Oogie was paraded before the villagers. Danh explained the situation and asked for feedback from his neighbours. The war had had no effect on these people. Cao Lanh was not located in a war zone so there was no animosity to the Australian.

One question from the village elder Mr Ngo was, lợi ích là gì? 'what's the benefit?'

Hanh explained that Oogie was an engineer who could help them become better organised.

A vote was taken and it was agreed the Australian could stay. Their decision would be reviewed in a month.

Oogie was pleased with the decision, as was Hahn, who had become close to the soldier.

Oogie knew he needed to impress the villagers with his engineering skills if he was to be allowed to stay in the village.

He walked around the grounds looking for a project to undertake, quite often with Binh beside him. On the very outskirts, he and Binh came across a broken-down motorcycle. On further examination, he discovered it was a 250cc Honda.

Cao Lanh was very close to the Mekong River, but it was located 200 metres from the river's edge to protect the village from flooding.

Water was carried by the women of the village in buckets balanced on a wooden pole. It was poured into a communal tank where the villagers would transfer the water into a bucket and transport it into their huts.

Women of Cao Lanh Carrying Water

A thought occurred to Oogie. What if he could get the motorcycle's motor going and modify it to become a water pump? He could then use bamboo pipes to pump the water up to the tank.

How to pipe the water into the huts would be eventually determined.

The young engineer began work. He extracted the motor and fashioned various plumbing parts out of bamboo. He used cooking oil as a substitute for petrol. Binh became Oogie's gofer, fetching various materials.

After a week he was ready to try out the pump. He kick-started the engine and it started on the fourth try. Water spewed out of the pipe attached. The villagers were fascinated but could not understand why the white man had built such a machine.

Oogie asked Hanh to organise the villagers to cut bamboo two inches in diameter. He needed over 200 metres in length.

Three days later the bamboo pipes had been joined using a native glue to make a line, 200 metres in all.

Oogie was hoping to have a test run privately, but that was not to be. All the villagers were waiting to see what the Australian soldier had achieved.

He kick-started the engine and she started the first time. The villagers could hear the water being pumped through the bamboo pipes. Binh raced to the tank and yelled out. 'nước chảy vào bể. Water is flowing into the tank.'

No one was more delighted than the water carriers.

Oogie designed and built a junction box which pumped water into six huts. Each hut had a container that would, when filled, stop the water flow with an improvised ball and cock system. The pipes would then be moved onto the next six huts and so on.

The young engineer was a hero and there was no dispute he would be allowed to stay permanently in the village. He and his apprentice Binh became inseparable.

Oogie became part of the village population and as such was expected to contribute in every way, including working in the rice fields. It was backbreaking work but Oogie enjoyed the camaraderie. His relationship with Hanh had grown stronger and stronger and marriage had been discussed.

It had been two years since the hydro project, and Oogie decided it was time for another project.

The scheme that stood out was also the most labour-intensive; a traditional communal house.

The village did have a communal house but it was dilapidated and hardly used by the villagers.

Oogie approached the village elder, Mr Ngo, to seek his approval. He agreed to call a meeting of the villagers so they could decide. The village assembled in front of the old communal house where Mr Ngo explained the proposal and asked his people to vote. They weren't just voting on a new communal house; they were deciding to contribute significant labour to the project.

The vote was overwhelmingly in favour and the project could begin.

The first step was to design the structure and create workable blueprints.

Once the design was completed, the materials were milled from the jungle. The outside walls were to be constructed using mud bricks.

There was a dedicated team to perform each task. As 20,000 bricks were required, most of the villagers were dedicated to this task.

Oogie was not only the architect and project leader; he was a labourer, a carpenter and a brickie.

The building took nine months to construct, and by the end of it Cao Lanh had the best communal house in South Vietnam.

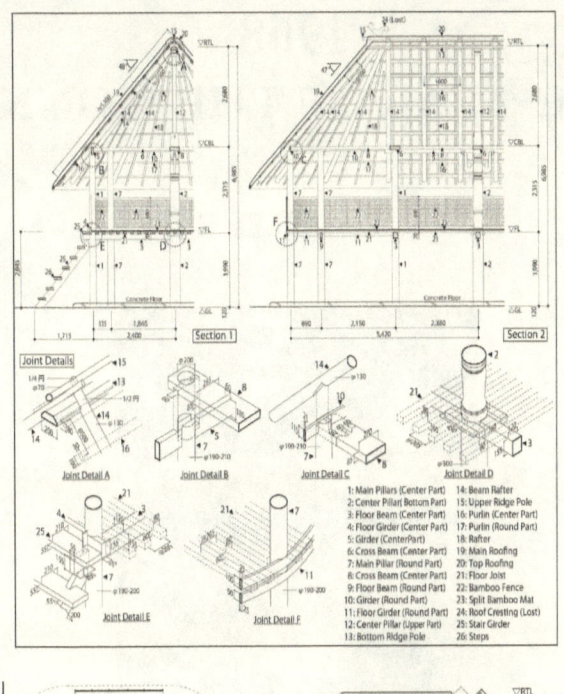

Figure 6: Application of units in floor plan and cross-sectional plan in Thuong Quang Commune

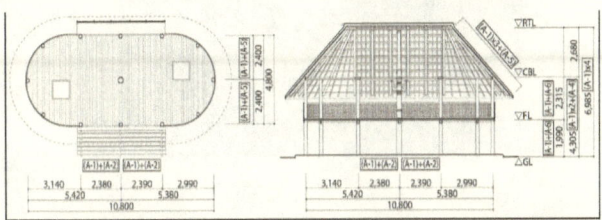

Cao Lanh Communal House

1968
THE YEAR OF THE MONKEY

CHAPTER 5

The Tet Offensive was launched in late January, 1968. Tet signifies the Chinese New Year, and 1968 was the year of the monkey. The Viet Cong launched the offensive, and it marked a significant escalation in the scale and the intensity of the Vietnam War. Although the VC was defeated in a military sense, the Tet Offensive shook the resolve of the Americans and their allies in Vietnam, and fuelled anti-war sentiment in America and the rest of the world.

Anti-War Demonstration San Francisco

In 1967, factions within the Viet Cong and North Vietnamese leadership began to call for a change in the way the war was being conducted.

General Vo Nguyen Giap, who had formerly advocated waging a largely guerrilla war, came to believe a "quick victory" might now be possible.

General Vo Nguyen Giap

The war cabinet agreed with the General and planning began for a major offensive in South Vietnam that would provoke a general uprising against the corrupt and unpopular South Vietnamese Government. Abandoning conventional military tactics, Viet Cong forces were not heavily concentrated for the offensive. The aim, instead, was to mount as many different attacks in as many locations as possible. And in a departure from the norm, the main targets were in population centres rather than the countryside.

Tet Offensive Saigon

January 28 1968

Oogie had decided that the communal house would benefit from electricity. Lights could be installed and a record player could entertain the villagers. There was no electrical connection to Cao Lanh and the closest substation was 100 kilometres away. He decided the only practical way to achieve his objective was to purchase a generator.

The villagers did have a fund for special purchases such as farming equipment. Oogie approached the village elder and explained the benefits of a generator to the village. After much discussion, he agreed to release the required funds from the kitty.

Oogie couldn't go into Saigon so it was decided Hahn would go.

The journey would take a day and she had a donkey and cart to transport the generator back to the village.

Hanh enjoyed the time out of the village. It was a beautiful day of 28 degrees and blue skies. Her intention was to stay the night just outside Saigon on a cousin's farm and then ride into Saigon the next morning.

Hanh enjoyed the evening with her cousin Chi with whom she used to play when they were children.

The next morning, she hitched up the donkey and bade farewell to Chi and her family. The distance to Saigon was quite short. She estimated it would take her an hour. She found the shop where the generator was being held for her. She was in the shop paying the man when she heard rapid gunshots and loud yelling.

The shop was close to the American Embassy and Hahn could see many black clad Viet Cong firing their rifles at the building. This was Hanh's first taste of war and she didn't like it.

She was caught between a rock and a hard place. She couldn't go out into the street for fear of being caught in the crossfire. The shop owner made it clear to her that there was not enough room for her to stay with his family. Finally, as the battle raged on, he decided she could sleep on the floor of the shop.

Aftermath of US Embassy Attack

Hanh was able to leave the next morning along with the much-anticipated generator, and she returned to her village without being attacked.

'Thank God you've returned safely! Even we in the village heard that Saigon had been attacked. Are you all right, my love?'

'Yes, I'm fine although it was scary. I saw several dead bodies on the grass in front of the embassy.'

'We are insulated here so we sometimes forget there's a war going on.'

'Not any more.'

Oogie seconded a couple of the men to lift the generator out of the cart and place it on the wooden platform he had built for that purpose beside the communal house.

He had already erected lights in the house so it was all ready to go. It was just a matter of firing up the generator, which he did on the first pull of the cord. The lights blinked a few times and then shone brightly. When the villagers all came into the communal house, they thought it was a miracle.

That night musical instruments were played under the magical light provided by the generator.

'Wait until we get the record player and some records! They won't know themselves,' said Oogie.

'You have done so much for this village, Oogie. I can't thank you enough,' said Hahn.

'I know how you can thank me, my darling.'

'Oh yes, and how's that?'

'You can marry me.'

'It would be my honour.'

'Excellent, when?'

'Let me speak to my parents first.'

'Okay, but do it soon.'

BLACK IS THE NEW BLACK

CHAPTER 6

Life was good for Oogie and Hanh. The Australian had asked for Hahn's hand in marriage and permission had been granted. They planned to marry in the spring of 1970.

Oogie had become a well respected member of the village, not only because of his engineering skills but also for his overall contribution to the life of the village.

Cao Lanh had avoided the tragedy of war thus far but that was about to change.

21 February 1970

It was early in the morning and the villagers were going about their business feeding the poultry and pigs. The water pump was started to ensure the water supply was sufficient for the day's usage.

Breakfast was being prepared by the women for their families in the normal morning ritual.

Binh ran into the village from where he'd been fishing on the banks of the river.

'Soldiers are coming, soldiers are coming.'

Oogie had dug a bunker in Hahn's family's hut where he lived. It was well disguised and was provisioned well enough for him to remain hidden for a week. Hahn helped him in and pulled the rug over the trapdoor.

The villagers stopped what they were doing and assembled in front of the communal house.

The soldiers were a platoon of Viet Cong operatives led by Captain Pham.

He announced to the villagers that the war against the American aggressors was going to plan. Vietnam would soon be reunified, but the Viet Cong required more recruits to help win the day.

He acknowledged that Cao Lanh was a small village and couldn't provide all its eligible recruits.

'All men and women aged between 18 and 25 are required to step forward.'

Hahn was 21, so she stepped forward.

'I will tap on the shoulder of every fifth person. Step forward if you are tapped.'

Hanh was tapped on the shoulder. She would become a proud member of the Viet Cong. There was no opportunity to say goodbye to Oogie. She said goodbye to her parents and her little brother. She knew the chances of seeing them again were remote.

Hanh and her fellow Cao Lanh recruits were marched to the Cu Chi district. This Viet Cong stronghold was located just 40 kilometres from Saigon in an area called the Iron Triangle. This was an area covering 310 square kilometres in the Bình Dương Province. It was so named because it was a stronghold of the Viet Cong.

Underneath the jungle terrain lay the most complex labyrinth of sophisticated tunnels. These tunnels were the backbone of the Viet Cong stronghold that defended the VC base, which was used as a base for attacks on Saigon and its surroundings. The most extensive tunnel system lay north of the village Cu Chi. It covered over 400 kilometres.

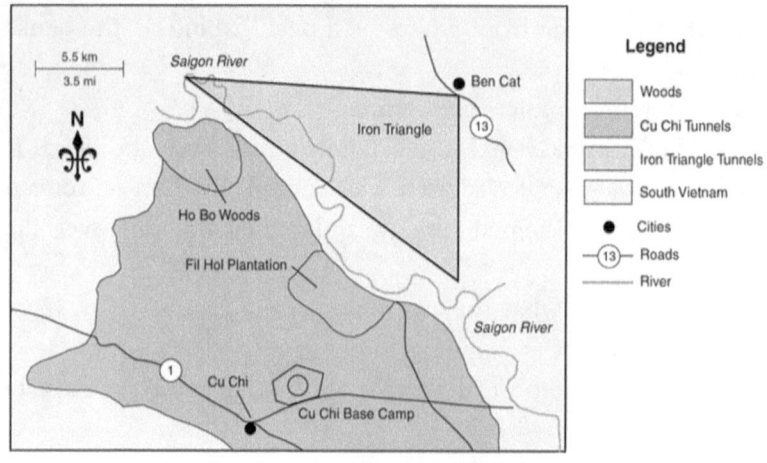

Viet Cong Tunnel Complex

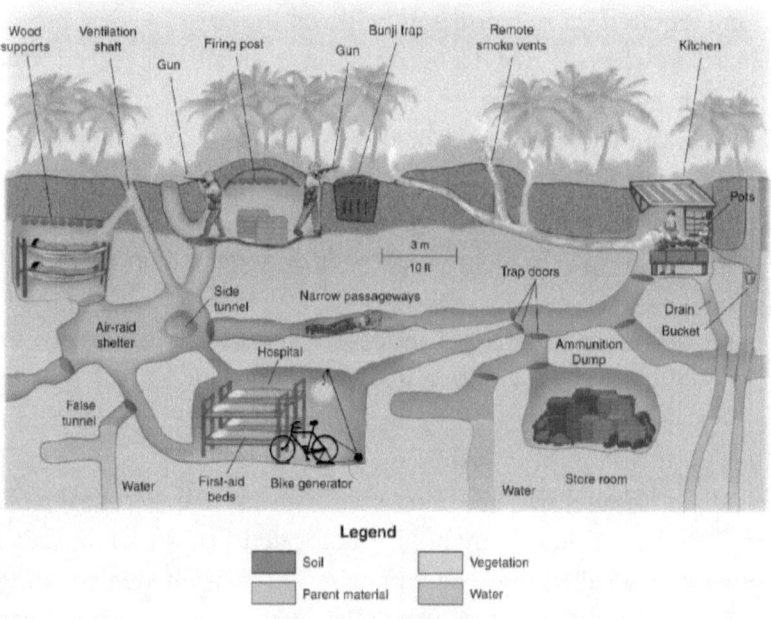

The Viet Cong tunnel network contained living areas, storage depots, ordnance factories, and hospitals. This extensive tunnel network enabled the VC to wage war against America and her allies for many years.

It was here that Hanh was headquartered to conduct her sniper activities.

Hanh was appointed a sniper during her training. Her instructors were amazed at her accuracy with the AK47.

Hahn, Viet Cong Sniper

The Viet Cong were able to secure weapons from the U.S and allied forces after a battle. These weapons were then used against their original owners.

One of the most prized weapons was a sniper's rifle.

The rifle allocated to Hahn had been heavily modified to suit its purpose. Those modifications included a free-floating barrel, a bolt-on silencer, Harris bi-pod front legs, retooling to make it fire a .338 round, an enlarged and retooled ejector port, a fibreglass stock instead of the standard wooden stock, and a foam-filled leather pouch strapped to the butt-stock that, in essence, formed a cheek rest.

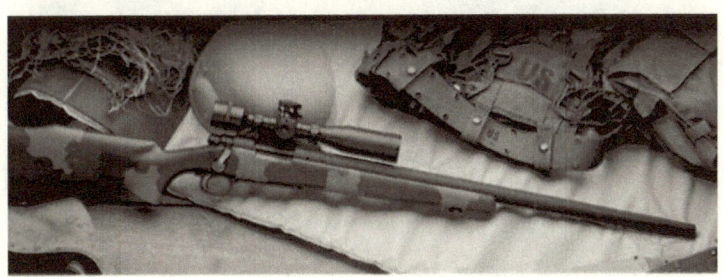

Hahn used the network of tunnels very effectively. Her comrades would inform her when enemy soldiers were on the move. She would lie in wait until she had a Sergeant or higher rank in her sights. She only ever fired one bullet. She would then hurry back to the well-camouflaged trap door and re-enter the tunnels.

Camouflaged entrance

Entrance to tunnel system

The most infamous of the snipers was also a woman. The Americans called her Apache.

Her specialty was to wound the enemy then torture them within earshot of their platoon. She cut off eyelids and held them in a pouch hanging from her belt. She castrated many a soldier and left him to bleed to death.

Hahn detested this woman and would have nothing to do with her.

At the end of her two-year conscription, she returned to her village, hoping Oogie was still living there. He was.

In the meantime, Apache was going about her cruel business. The US Marines had many snipers in its service but none better than the "white feather", Carlos Hathcock. He took out this cruel bitch with one shot. He shot her a second time just to make sure.

Apache Woman

Carlos The White Feather

BOMBS IN THE SKY

CHAPTER 7

December 1972

Washington DC

Richard Nixon was sitting at the famous Resolute Desk. Many presidents before him and after him sat at the same desk with pride.

Nixon had hoped to end the Vietnam War by now but things were not going America's way.

His foray into Laos the previous year to destroy the Ho Chi Minh trail had failed miserably.

He was being advised by his Secretary of State, William Rogers.

John Ehrlichman and his Defence Minister Melvin Laird advised that the only way to beat the communists was to bomb the living daylights out of them.

Operation Linebacker was devised to drop over 20,000 tons of high explosive over predominantly Hanoi to break the enemy's spirit.

Café Pho Co

Hang Buom and his wife Ha ran a café, Café Pho Co, in the centre of Hanoi. Their two children, Chi a twelve-year-old girl, and An, a fourteen-year-old boy, helped their parents when they were not attending school.

'I'm hopeful this wretched war will be over soon. The Paris peace talks have been going for some time now,' said Hang Buom.

'I hope you are right. my husband. Who can forget the bombing of 1966? I was sure we would all die.'

'It looks like a good crowd today. Maybe the Christians are out celebrating Christmas.'

'True, do you know how many Christians there are in Vietnam?'

'About seven million, apparently.'

'Chi asked me if she will receive a present for Christmas this year.'

'What did you tell her?'

'I explained we are communists and don't believe in Jesus.'

'How did she take it?'

'Pretty well. She just wanted a new dress. She didn't care about Christmas or Jesus.'

'When they both get home from school we'll treat them to a special cake.'

December 18 1972

Guam Pacific

Captain Gary Woods briefed his five-man crew before take-off.

'Okay, boys, we are next to take off. We and the 86 other bombers are heading for Hanoi. We intend to blow the living daylights out of the Commies. If that doesn't make them surrender nothing will.'

The bomber force took six hours and fourteen minutes to reach Hanoi and began dropping over 20,000 tons of bombs.

Bomb Hits Hanoi

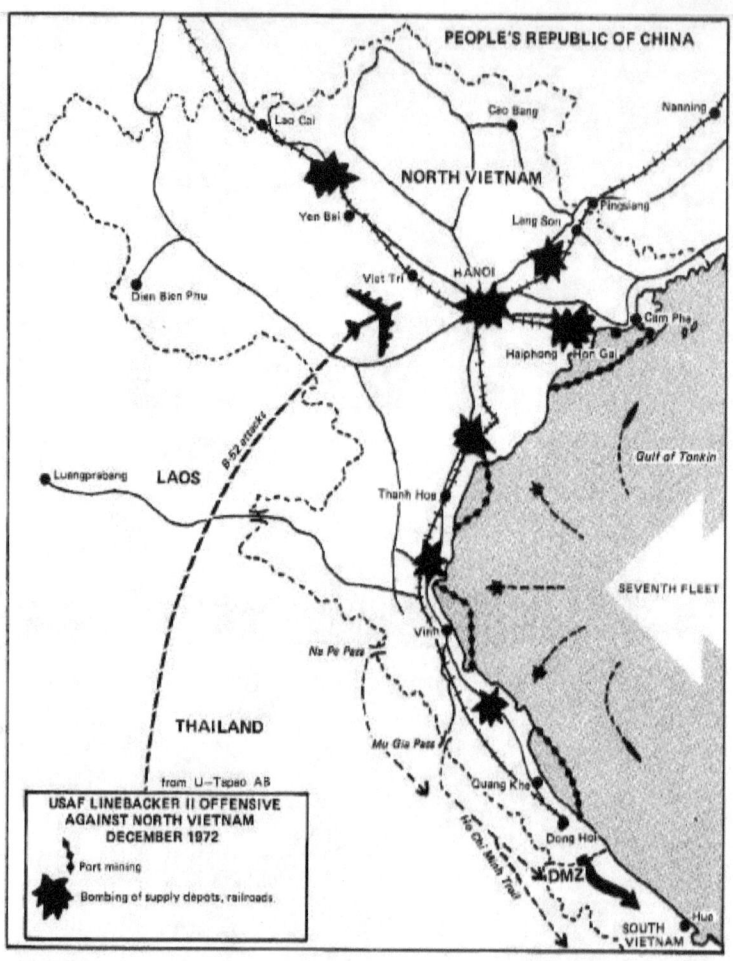

An and Chi were walking home from school when An stopped in his tracks.

'What's wrong, An?'

'Look up. What do you see?'

'Oh no.'

The two children saw American bombers blotting out the sky. Bombs began to fall on their beloved city. They ran to a Catholic church, hoping they would be safe.

The bombing lasted well over an hour and when the bombardment finished, An and Chi returned to their parents' café and home. As they approached their neighbourhood they realised it had been largely destroyed. They turned the corner and stared at the devastation they couldn't recognise as the café. They scrambled as fast as they could over the bombed-out buildings until they reached what they believed was their home. Their mother and father lay among the rubble. Both were dead.

A soldier approached the siblings and asked if they had a family. They informed him both their parents had been killed in the bombing.

'Do you have any living relatives?'

'We have an uncle who lives on a farm on the outskirts of Hanoi,' answered An.

'Come and show me where.'

An and Chi and the soldier made their way to the children's uncle's farm. Both children sobbed most of the way.

Total Destruction

They walked five miles, reaching Uncle Huynh's house at dusk.

Huynh was regarded as a wealthy farmer in the region, as his farm measured 100 acres whereas most farms in the area were 10 acres or less.

'You two stay here while I talk to your uncle,' said Duc, the soldier.

'Hello, is there anybody home?'

There was no answer. Duc yelled louder. Finally, a distinctive looking man appeared.

'Who are you? I don't recall inviting anybody here tonight.'

'Excuse me, sir, but I have a most important subject to discuss with you.'

Duc explained what had happened to the children's parents and how he, their uncle, was their only living relative.

'I had two sons. Both were killed in the war. I don't believe I could take care of the children. I suggest you find them a suitable orphanage in Hanoi.'

'Your niece and nephew will be mortified. They have not only lost their parents, but they are now being rejected by their only living kin.'

'I have my reasons.'

Duc explained to the children that their uncle did not have room for them.

'Come, we will find an orphanage where you will be able to stay. They will look after you both.'

The only orphanage Duc knew was the Hanoi Orphanage. He led the children to the building that housed the institution. Duc was relieved to discover the building was undamaged.

He needed to return to barracks as he had already been away too long.

'I'm leaving you here. Just knock on the front door and explain your situation. Good luck.'

Ha[son] did as Duc instructed and an older lady opened the door and ushered them in. After hearing their story she accepted them both as orphans.

Dormitory

WAR'S END

CHAPTER 8

Le Duc Tho & Henry Kissinger shake on the peace agreement

As part of the Accord, North Vietnam returned 591 American prisoners of war. Operation Homecoming was completed.

Oogie and Hanh were aware of these developments, as Hanh still had a close relationship with senior Viet Cong operatives. Oogie had finally come to grips with the fact Hanh was a key member of the organisation he once considered the enemy. He was now of the view that it was the U.S. and its allies such as Australia who were the aggressors. The Vietnamese just wanted a unified country and to be left in peace.

WAR
WHAT'S IT GOOD FOR?

CHAPTER 9

April 1975

The Fall of Saigon

The Vietnamese people had been occupied by foreign powers since 1887 when Napoleon III imposed a colonial system on Vietnam.

Now at last Vietnam was unified under one flag and one Government.

At what cost?

- Two million civilians killed from both North and South Vietnam.
- One million North Vietnamese and Viet Cong soldiers killed.
- Two hundred and fifty thousand South Vietnamese Soldiers killed.
- Fifty-eight thousand U.S. soldiers killed.
- Five hundred and twenty-one Australian soldiers killed.

A new era begins

At last Oogie could be seen outside the village of Cao Lanh, albeit he was known as a French Vietnamese citizen.

He had purchased a Singer sewing machine just before the end of the war and he hoped he and Hanh would become proficient sewers. With plenty of practice, they both became skilled at the craft.

Oogie suggested to Hanh that they establish a clothing label and sell their clothes to the public. She was enthusiastic about the idea they decided to name their label, "Oogie".

Oogie was able to import fashion magazines from France and England. These magazines gave the two young entrepreneurs ideas for their own designs.

The Oogie brand began to establish a name for good quality clothing at a reasonable price. As demand grew, so too did the workload.

The couple began employing people from their village and so the Oogie Fashion workforce was established.

The financial plan they agreed upon was to distribute 50% of the profits back to the village after wages and taxes had been paid.

The remainder would be used to expand the company and pay Oogie and Hanh a reasonable salary.

Vietnam was becoming a safe place to live. No more war, no more bombing, mantraps, battles and torture. What still existed were land mines and unexploded bombs. Many thousands of Vietnamese citizens would lose their lives or their legs well after the war ended.

Oogie and Hanh made the decision to establish a charity to support those families who lost loved ones and those citizens who were maimed. They called it the Aura Foundation. An instrumental part of the foundation's work was employing people to sweep known landmine areas with sophisticated detection devices including trained rats.

Clearing Landmines

Unexploded Shells

Largest Unexploded Bomb Found in Vietnam

This shell was fired from the U.S. Battleship New Jersey.

The New Jersey fired 5,688 16-Inch Shells during the Vietnam War.

Oogie and Hanh had been trying to start a family for over two years. Vietnam still did not have an IVF program, and it seemed the only alternative was to travel to Australia. Oogie was concerned that as far as the Australian authorities were concerned Private Ian Jones was MIA and presumed dead. He didn't possess an Australian passport; in fact, he didn't possess a Vietnamese passport. They faced a serious conundrum.

The company had been operating for five years and was profitable from the outset. Cao Lanh had benefited greatly. Several new homes had been built, all with running water and electricity. Several more were planned. Oogie and Hanh were highly respected in the community.

The government also supported the two entrepreneurs and the amount of tax they collected from Oogie Fashions was significant.

ROUGE THE COLOUR OF BLOOD

CHAPTER 10

*"We will burn the old grass and the new will grow." – **Pol Pot***

1925 Prek Sbauv Cambodia

Both mother and father were happy that their eighth child had been born a healthy bouncing baby boy. They named him Saloth Sar. His father, Pen Saloth, and his mother, Sok Nem, were prominent members of the village and considered wealthy with 50 acres of rice paddies whereas the average villager owned 10.

Saloth attended school in a Buddhist monastery and then a French Catholic School. Initially, he decided that carpentry would be his career, but he was offered a scholarship in Paris where he was regarded as a clever and dutiful student.

Saloth joined the communist party soon after arriving in Paris. He adopted the philosophies of Stalin and Mao Zedong.

In 1953, he returned to Cambodia and immediately joined the Khmer Viet Minh; a Marxist-Leninist driven organisation.

His first taste of war was fighting a guerrilla campaign against King Norodom Sihanouk.

King Sihanouk 1953

Saloth moved to North Vietnam, teaming up with the Viet Cong living in the jungle. He was impressed with Hanoi during his many visits and he also visited Beijing. This would be one of many visits to China.

Saloth's standing in the Communist Party was rising. He was appointed the general secretary of the Communist Party of Kampuchea in 1963. It was at this time that he began his frequent visits to Beijing. Mao's Cultural Revolution particularly impressed him. While in Beijing he was trained by several high-ranking officials of the Communist Party of China.

Shaming in China

Saloth adopted the name Pol Pot. It was a name which would go down in infamy.

China provided 90% of the foreign aid pouring into Cambodia. China also lent Pol Pot's Government $1 Billion interest-free, which was spent on military aid.

This enabled Pol Pot to seize power and instigate his evil plan for Cambodia.

The Killing Fields 1975

Pol Pot

Pol Pot and the Khmer Rouge, after consulting with their mentor Mao Zedong, decided they would turn the country into a socialist agrarian republic.

The first stage was to empty all the cities and relocate the population into labour camps in the rural regions.

Here they were expected to produce an average national yield of 1.4 tons of rice per acre. Workers were forced to labour for twelve-hour days to meet these impossible demands. Often, they worked without being properly fed and on an insufficient amount of rest.

Cambodian Labour Camp

By January 1979, between 2 and 3 million people died at the hands of Pol Pot and the Khmer Rouge.

It is estimated that over 20,000 people entered but did not leave the S21 prison in Phnom Pen, one of 196 torture centres operated by the Khmer Rouge.

All S21 prisoners were photographed

Victims were driven in trucks to the killing fields where they were slaughtered with various instruments such as pick handles. Bullets were not wasted on the unfortunate victims.

It is estimated that 60% of the citizens died from execution. The remainder died from starvation and disease.

The Khmer Rouge initially ordered the expulsion of ethnic Vietnamese from Cambodia, but large numbers of that population were massacred as they attempted to flee the country. The regime then prevented the remaining 20,000 ethnic Vietnamese from fleeing. The Khmer Rouge slaughtered them.

Additionally, the Khmer Rouge conducted many cross-border raids into Vietnam where they murdered an estimated 30,000 Vietnamese civilians. Most notably, during the Ba Chúc massacre in April 1978, the Khmer Rouge military crossed the border and entered the Ba Chúc village, slaughtering 3,157 Vietnamese civilians. This forced an urgent response from the Vietnamese government, precipitating the Cambodian–Vietnamese War.

Cao Lanh Vietnam

January 1979

Christmas Day 1978

While the Christian world celebrated the birth of Jesus Christ, 140,000 Vietnamese troops invaded Democratic Kampuchea and overran the Kampuchean Revolutionary Army. The Vietnamese succeeded in just two weeks. The invasion halted the excesses of Pol Pot's regime, which had been responsible for the deaths of almost half of all Cambodians between 1975 and December 1978. Vietnamese military intervention enabled international food aid to be distributed, mitigating the massive famine and ending the Cambodian genocide.

Vietnam Soldiers Enter Phnom Pen

Viet Soldiers Invade Phnom Penh

Binh and his parents were prepared for the young man to be conscripted into the army as every male-aged from 18 to 27 must serve in the military.

Binh travelled to Ho Chi Minhh City to register for service. Because of the war with Cambodia, he was required to remain in the army for five years.

Binh in Cambodia

WELCOME HOME

CHAPTER 11

1980

Melbourne

Oogie was keen to return home to Australia, and not only for business reasons. He looked forward to catching up with his old friends including Rosco. He also wanted to visit his parents' grave at Melbourne Central Cemetery in Carlton.

Cemetery with Melbourne City in the Background

The couple decided to call in some favours from the government. Oogie was granted a Vietnamese passport and they only needed an appropriate visa to be granted by the Australian Government.

After some toing-and-froing with the Australian Embassy, the French Vietnamese gentleman and the Vietnamese lady were granted visas for three months.

Oogie was amused that his Vietnamese passport had him listed as Oogie Jones.

Hanh was conscious of the fact that her young brother, Binh, had been conscripted into the Vietnamese Army and was now serving in

Cambodia. She also knew there was nothing she or Oogie could do to change that. They both agreed the trip should go ahead. She prayed for his safety every night.

Melbourne February 1981

When Oogie and Hanh landed in Melbourne, the temperature was 30 degrees with 80% humidity and it felt just like home.

Oogie had booked a room at the Windsor Hotel; a classic hotel that he had always admired but never thought he would be able to afford to stay in.

The hotel was a short tram ride from the cemetery, and they planned to make the trip the following day.

Oogie had written to Ross's parents requesting their son's address and telephone number. They wrote back immediately with the details.

Once the couple had settled into their suite, Oogie tried calling his old university friend.

The telephone rang for what seemed an eternity. Oogie was about to hang up when he heard a female voice.

'Hargraves residence; can I help you?'

'Oh, hello, this is Oogie Jones. I wonder if Ross would be available?'

'He's in the garage; if you hold on I'll get him for you. What was your name again?'

'Oogie, but he also knows me as Ian Jones.'

'I see. Just wait and I'll get him for you.'

Oogie waited for five minutes. It seemed like fifty and he was tempted to hang up and forget the whole thing. Maybe too much water had passed under the bridge.

'Are you kidding me? How the fuck are you, you bastard?'

'Well, that's a nice greeting after fifteen fucking years, mate.'

'I've been expecting to hear from you since Mum and Dad told me you were alive and coming home.'

'Well let's get together, and I can fill you in on the last decade and a half. Are you free tomorrow night?'

'We are, but we would like you to come here and have dinner with us?'

'I'm sure that would be fine. I'll just run it past Hanh and call you back. Is that okay?'

'Yeah, that's fine. I take it Hanh is your wife?'

'Yes, she is. You'll like her.'

'Okay, mate, call me back.'

Oogie consulted with Hanh and she was enthusiastic about meeting Oogie's old friend. He rang Ross back.

'All good, Rosco. What's your address, mate?'

'We're at 231 St Georges Road Toorak.'

'Holy hell, you've come up in the world.'

'Yes, I've done all right. We can talk about it when we see you. Come at about 6.30.'

'Done, see you then.'

Hanh had listened into the telephone conversation with interest.

'Oogie, why were you surprised by Ross's address?'

'He is living in one of the most prestigious addresses in Melbourne. He must have made a lot of money in the last fifteen years and I suspect it wasn't by doing tax returns.'

'Well, I suppose we will hear tomorrow night.'

Hanh and Oogie spent the day visiting recommended fashion agents. Appointing a good agent was fundamental to their label's success.

They met with four agents. All of them were keen to represent the Oogie brand, but one stood out. His name was John Brodie, and his company was called JB Fashions. Hanh and Oogie agreed to meet with John the next day to agree on terms.

Oogie asked the hotel's concierge to organise a taxi for 6.15 and they arrived at Ross and his wife Loretta's house right on time.

231 St Georges Road Toorak

Ian rang the doorbell. Within seconds, the door opened and Ross hugged his old mate and would not let go. Hahn and Loretta were left standing awkwardly.

'Hello, you must be Hahn. I'm Loretta. Pleased to meet you.'

'It's very nice to meet you, Loretta, and when your husband stops hugging mine I'll introduce you.'

'Oh, I'm sorry, ladies, but you must understand I thought Oogie was dead all this time; everybody did.'

'Of course, we understand it must be amazing. Let's all go inside and have a glass of champagne.'

The two couples entered the living room, which was beautifully decorated. Once the Dom Perignon champagne was served, they began conversing.

'Do you two have any children, Loretta?'

'Yes, we have a boy, Gregory who is fourteen, and a girl aged twelve. Her name is Jan. What about you two?'

'No, but we would like to. Part of the reason for visiting Melbourne was to see if we qualify for the IVF program.'

'Oh, good luck with it.'

'Thank you.'

'Ross, do you mind me asking how you became so wealthy? I didn't think accountants made so much.'

'No, I don't think they do generally. After a few years practising as an accountant, another client referred a truck driver to me. His name was Dave Hall; a nice hard-working fellow. I established a business relationship with Dave and we also became good friends. In 1975 he died of a melanoma. He was sixty-one and a bachelor, and he left his business to me.

'My initial response was to sell it, but that was more difficult than I initially envisaged.

'Loretta and I decided to continue operating the business until we found a buyer. As it turned out, the business grew and grew. I quit my accounting practice and became CEO of HIT Pty Ltd.'

'Why did you call it HIT?'

'That was the original name. It was an acronym for Hall's Interstate Transport. We changed it to Hargraves International Transport.'

'So how many trucks have you got running on the road, mate?'

'Two thousand, and growing.'

'My God, you're huge.'

'We are, and we also have one million square metres of warehousing space.'

'Do you operate in any other countries?'

Yeah, we do, in New Zealand and throughout Asia. We are looking at the USA at the moment.'

'Well, congratulations to you both. You took an opportunity and ran with it. You deserve the success you are both enjoying.'

'That's enough about us. We would love to hear your story.'

Ian recounted how he had been shot down in a Huey helicopter and captured by the Viet Cong. He told of the torture and the living conditions he had to endure and how he and others escaped into the jungle.

Hanh interrupted Oogie with her account of how she found the near-dead Australian soldier lying in a paddy field.

She told of hiding him and bringing him back to health and then introducing him to the village.

Oogie and Hahn continued with their story right up until the present. They did, however, omit the time Hanh was a sniper with the Viet Cong.

'Wow, you could write a book about your lives. What an amazing tale,' said Ross. 'So, you two; what brings you to Melbourne other than catching up with your very best friend… the friend who thought you were dead?'

'We have, as you know, developed a fashion brand in Vietnam. The response we have received from Singapore and Hong Kong has been amazing. We decided that we would try our hand in Australia. If we succeed here we will then look at Europe and the USA.'

'How do you envisage breaking into the Australian market, Oogie?'

'We will need a fashion agent. We met with four today and have selected a fellow we feel very comfortable with. His name is John Brodie and his company is JB Fashions.'

'I know I'm not in the fashion industry, but I do know a lot of people in this city. Would you like me to check him out so to speak?'

'I think that would be a good idea, Ross, thanks mate.'

'Another thought, Oogie. Loretta and I are very good friends with Ken and Ya Suko Myers and I am sure they would be happy to introduce you to their head fashion buyer. No promises but you never know. If you can crack Myers you will be well on your way.

'I also know John Spalvins, the David Jones CEO. They are one of our major clients. I could ask him if he could help you along.'

'Thank you so much. We appreciate your support.'

'If you can't help your good friends, who can you help? Let's have dinner. I have a special bottle of red you might like. It will go with the steak Chef has prepared.'

'You have a chef?'

'Only on special occasions such as this.'

1971 Grange Hermitage

The chef, Giorgio D'Nofrio, normally worked at Vlado's Steak House.

He prepared a superb Filet Poivre accompanied by string French fries, asparagus, and carrots. It was delicious. The wine complemented the meal.

The dessert was chocolate fondant with homemade vanilla ice cream.

The evening concluded with coffee and port... just not any port; a 1933 Para was served.

'May I interest you in a cigar and a fine malt whiskey to round off the evening, Oogie?'

'Is the Pope a Catholic?'

'We'll have it in my study. The girls will be all right for a little while on their own.'

'Sounds wonderful, Rosco.'

Ross poured the 25-year-old Macallan and offered a Montecristo cigar to his old friend.

'This is what I call living, Ross. This malt is magnificent.'

'It would want to be. It cost me $1200.'

'Holy shit.'

'So, Oogie, what do you think of Loretta?'

'She's lovely, mate. Where did you meet her?'

'Do you remember the night at the pub when we celebrated the end of University days?'

'Fucking oath I do. That was a great night. We both scored.'

'We sure did. it turned out I got my sheila pregnant that night. Her name was Loretta.'

'Well fuck me! You've been married to her for fifteen years.'

'Yeah, and I couldn't be happier.'

'Good on you mate.'

The evening came to an end with the two couples thoroughly enjoyed themselves.

Oogie and Hanh thanked their hosts and Ross called a taxi. They made arrangements to catch up again once Ross had contacted Ken Myer and John Spalvins.

WE'LL SAVE YOU

CHAPTER 12

When Vietnam rode in on white chargers to save what remained of the Cambodian population from Pol Pot and his evil forces, they were surprised at the world's reaction.

They installed a Khmer Rouge Army officer, Heng Samrin, as their leader. There were Vietnamese advisers at every Government level including Ministerial.

Vietnam's supporters included:

Soviet Union

Poland

Czechoslovakia
East Germany
Democratic Kampuchea (Khmer Rouge) Supporters
China
Thailand
Malaysia
Singapore
United Kingdom
United States
Australia

Binh proved himself to be a very capable soldier and he rose through the ranks rapidly. He was promoted to Captain in January 1979.

He was recalled from Cambodia soon after his promotion to defend his beloved country from the Chinese hordes invading from the north.

China invaded to force Vietnam to withdraw from its good ally, Cambodia.

Chinese crossing into Vietnam

China managed to capture several Vietnamese towns near the Chinese Vietnamese border.

Devastated Vietnamese Town

After three weeks and six days, China withdrew, claiming victory. Vietnam claimed they were driven out and they too claimed victory.

Binh was leading his men against the Chinese aggressor when a shell exploded very close to him. There was nothing left of him to bury.

Chinese Artillery

Hanh and her parents were not advised of Binh's demise until one year later.

Hanh was in Melbourne at the time, about to launch the Oogie brand.

Casualties

Chinese estimate: 6,954–8,531 killed. 14,800–21,000 wounded. 238 captured.

Vietnamese estimate: 62,000 casualties. (Including 26,000 killed) 420 tanks/APCs destroyed. 66 artillery pieces destroyed.

BUSINESS IS BUSINESS

CHAPTER 13

Oogie and Hahn decided they should visit the Myer and David Jones stores to ascertain the quality of the fashions they carried. They were impressed and they hoped both stores would carry the Oogie brand.

They returned to the Windsor and went to their suite, where the message light was showing on their telephone.

'Hello, this is Ian Jones in room 508. I believe there is a message for me?'

'Yes, Mr Jones. I'll have a bellboy bring it to your room straight away.'

Five minutes later the doorbell rang. Oogie answered it, took the message, and gave the bellboy an appropriate tip.

'Who's it from, darling?'

'It's from Ross. He has spoken to Ken Myer and John Spalvins. They have both agreed to meet with us and view a presentation of our range,' said Hahn.

'That's amazing! We were only expecting to meet with one of their fashion buyers. Meeting both Managing Directors is beyond all our dreams. Ross has done us proud,' said Oogie.

'The only issue now is can we impress them both?'

'Have faith, Hahn. We know our range is excellent. Just look at how successful we have been in Asia.'

'We need to hire a couple of top models,' said Hahn. 'Vivian's Modelling is regarded as the best in Melbourne.'

'Can I ask you to arrange the models?' asked Oogie.

'I'll visit the agency tomorrow. We need to find out when the presentation will be.'

'I'll speak to Mr Myers and Mr Spalvins' PAs and once we have a date locked in we can arrange for the models.

March 15 1981

Myers Board Room

Oogie and Hahn were nervously arranging the clothing they would be presenting to Mr Myers and his senior buyers. The models hadn't arrived yet. They were fifteen minutes late.

They arrived just in time and Hahn helped them dress in the first outfits, ready to stride out in front of the VIP audience.

By the end of the parade, Myers had committed to stock a full range of Oogie Fashions.

The same result occurred at David Jones. Oogie Fashions were well on their way to becoming a major fashion brand in Australia.

Oogie and Hahn decided to continue manufacturing in Vietnam, both for cost-effectiveness reasons and to provide employment opportunities for their people.

It didn't take long for boutiques in Melbourne to begin stocking the Oogie brand. Oogie became the hot fashion ticket. Albeit more slowly, the Sydney market also adopted the Oogie brand. DJs sold their first shipment in a few weeks. Double Bay and Neutral Bay boutiques stocked the brand, as did several city stores.

Melbourne Spring Parade Flemington Racecourse

November 1982

The organisers of the Melbourne Cup fashion parade were elated that they had been able to secure Elle McPherson and Christie Brinkley to headline the event at Flemington Racecourse. The event had become an integral part of the Spring Racing Carnival.

Oogie arrived back at the suite in the Windsor Hotel. He had been arranging what outfits would be worn in the parade. It had been agreed that Oogie Fashions would have four outfits worn on the catwalk.

'Hello darling, I've had a successful afternoon. We will have four outfits in the parade.'

'That's good, sweetheart. I too have had a win.'

'Oh?'

'I've been asked to model one of our outfits in "Fashions on the Field".'

'That's great! Just imagine if you won – the publicity would be fantastic.'

'Let's not get ahead of ourselves. The competition will be tough. Besides, I'm not sure I will be able to take part.'

'Why the heck not, Hahn?'

'We have a very important fashion show to organise, remember?'

'I can handle it. Besides, there are two hours between the events.'

'Okay, as long as you feel comfortable.'

'No problem, darling.'

Myer Fashions on the Field had established its place as Australia's largest and most prestigious outdoor fashion event, attracting media attention and celebrity judges from around the globe.

The competition was first staged in 1962 in a bid to attract more women to the male-dominated racecourse. Heats and finals for women, men, children, families, fashion designers and milliners stretched across the four days of the Melbourne Cup Carnival.

Myer Fashions on the Field was staged in an impressive two-storey enclosure located in Flemington's renowned fashion and entertainment quarter; the Park, situated on the hill behind the Flemington Grandstand.

The Melbourne Cup was the most important and popular horse race in Australia. With a history that went back to 1861, this magnificent event truly had become "the race that stops a nation". Held over a distance of 3200 metres, the Melbourne Cup had become Australia's most loved, most traditional, and most valuable thoroughbred horse race in Australia.

'Come on darling, if we don't leave soon we'll miss the cup altogether,' said Oogie.

'I won't be long. I'm having trouble with my hat.'

'Can I help?'

'I don't think so, darling. Millenary is not your forte.'

'Our taxi is due any minute, so you'd better get a move on.'

'There. How do I look?'

'I'm speechless. You look stunning, Hahn. If you don't win there is something terribly wrong.'

'I think you might be a little biased, darling, but thank you for the compliment.'

The Vietnamese couple arrived at Flemington Racecourse after a fifteen-minute cab ride from the Windsor. The taxi pulled up at the most famous address in Melbourne; 448 Epsom Rd, Flemington.

They had arranged to meet Ross and Loretta at the magnificent Atrium Restaurant.

They presented their tickets and entered the restaurant, and Ross waved them over to their table.

'Hello, you two. You both look absolutely splendid.'

'Thank you, Ross, you both look pretty splendid yourselves,' said Hahn.

'You're wearing a beautiful outfit, Hahn. I take it that is an Oogie Fashions design?'

'It is, Loretta. I've entered "Fashion on the Field". I'm naturally hoping I'll win. It would be great publicity for our label.'

'Well, I may not be a judge, but I think you're a shoo-in,' said Ross.

'Thank you, Ross, but it's not you I need to impress; it's the judges.'

Ross ordered a bottle of Moet. Once their glasses were charged; he proposed a toast.

'To the winner of Fashions on the Field; Hahn Jones.

'Who have you picked as a winner, Oogie?' he added, changing the subject.

'Kingston Town. I know he's the favourite and favourites rarely win the Melbourne Cup, but I have a gut feeling about him.'

'You could do a lot worse, mate. I'm going for Noble Comment. No particular reason other than I like the name.'

'What about you ladies?'

'I'm backing Gurner's Lane,' said Hahn.

'That's the horse I'm backing,' said Loretta.

'Why Gurner's Lane?'

'I like the colours,' said Hahn.

'Me too,' said Loretta.

'Okay, why don't we go down to the bookies' betting ring and place our bets.'

'That's an excellent idea, Oogie. I need to be ready for the Fashions on the Field by 9.30. It begins at 10 am.'

Without any particular reason, the group chose Roy Ranelagh as the bookie that would win them a small fortune.

They each placed $50 on their horse of choice. They all received a betting ticket and returned to the Atrium.

Hahn made her way down to the catwalk. There were sixteen contestants in all. They all looked like winners to her. She did not rate her chances highly.

Hahn was allocated number 16.

Oh great, I'm last. What chance have I got? she thought.

The fashion show began, hosted by a young media personality called Ita Buttrose.

As Hahn waited at the back of the marquee, she felt extremely nervous. Finally, it was her turn to walk the catwalk. She received generous applause.

The sixteen contestants had a fifteen-minute wait before Ita announced the winner... Mrs Hahn Jones wearing an Oogie Fashions original.

Hahn could not believe it. She accepted the prize; a trip for two to Paris.

Oogie greeted her when she stepped down from the catwalk with a huge hug. 'You did it, darling. I'm so proud of you.'

'Thank you, sweetheart, I can't believe it.'

The four friends returned to the Atrium and shared another bottle of champagne. This time it was a Dom Perignon. They all ate a light lunch.

At 2.30 pm, they decided to go down to the ring and inspect their horses. All three thoroughbreds looked magnificent. The other twenty-one looked pretty good also.

Once satisfied they had picked a winner, they returned to the Atrium to watch the race.

As the horses were led into the starters' gate, a couple were reluctant to enter. Once they were all in, the starter opened the gates and the 1982 Melbourne Cup began. Twenty-four racehorses took off on their 3200-metre journey to glory.

It was a close race, and the sound of hooves on the turf was exciting the crowd.

As the field approached the 3000-metre mark it was obvious the winner would be either Kingston Town or Gurner's Lane.

Gurner's Lane won by a neck. Mick Dittman, the jockey, rode a fantastic race.

The two ladies were beyond excitement. When things settled down, they returned to the bookies' ring to collect their winnings of $400.

Hahn couldn't believe her luck. She won Fashions on the Field and she backed the winner! Melbourne Cup Day would remain her favourite day of the year. The trip to Paris was for two. She and Oogie could be able to discover if their brand would be suitable in the fashion capital of the world.

They decided to travel the following March, at the beginning of the northern spring.

Hahn and Oogie's next appointment was at Melbourne IVF.

They had arranged a visit at the Parkville Clinic close to the Melbourne CBD.

Hahn and Oogie were nervous, as they were aware that the success rate for IVF was 20% to 30%. Several consultations included:

- Preimplantation genetic diagnosis to test embryos for specific genetic or chromosomal variations
- Preimplantation genetic screening, also known as PGT-A, to screen all 24 chromosomes in a developing embryo and selectively implant only the ones that are chromosomally healthy
- Time-lapse analysis to record the development of embryos and identify those more likely to result in a pregnancy
- Complementary and adjuvant IVF therapies that may be considered during IVF treatment to improve pregnancy success, particularly in women with repeated IVF failure
- Donor program including egg, embryo, sperm and surrogacy

Finally, an egg was inserted. They then had to wait fourteen days to determine if Hahn had become pregnant. She hadn't. The couple were devastated. They tried again the following month, again without success.

'Hahn, do you think we should try adopting a Vietnamese child?'

'I would like to try one more time. If it is unsuccessful we should consider adopting.'

The following month produced the same result.

GAY PARIS

CHAPTER 14

Hahn and Oogie flew to Paris at the beginning of February 1983. Neither had been to the City of Lights before. Although bitterly disappointed with the IVF program, they looked forward to adopting a child.

The couple checked into the Champ Elysees Plaza. Once rested, they searched for a restaurant. They chose Le Gabriel; a five-star establishment.

'What time is our appointment with the agent tomorrow, darling?' asked Hahn.

'Ten. I'm looking forward to meeting the principal. He's regarded as one of the most influential men in the French fashion industry.'

'What's his name? Forgive me for not knowing… I've had other things on my mind lately.'

'I understand, my love. His name is Marc Merklen, and the agency is "My Fashion Agent".'

'I should be able to remember that.'

Hahn and Oogie retired to bed early. It had been a long day, including a fourteen-hour flight from Melbourne.

The following afternoon, the two fashion designers made their way to the offices of My Fashion Agent. Oogie carried a portfolio of their most recent designs.

Oogie gave the taxi driver the address, 27 Rue Notre Dame de Nazareth.

They introduced themselves to the receptionist who invited them to take a seat on a leather lounge.

Marc's PA guided them to the boardroom ten minutes later. Marc was sitting at the end of the walnut table.

'Welcome to our agency, Hahn and Oogie. I've been looking forward to meeting you both. Please take a seat. You are the first Vietnamese designers I have met. I am keen to see your designs.'

'It's great to meet you, Marc. We have brought a portfolio of our most recent designs if you would care to take a look at them.'

Oogie and Hahn laid the large portfolio on the table in front of Marc. He began to turn the pages without making a comment. The two designers were worried. Surely, Marc would be impressed with at least some of their designs.

Marc closed the book once he had reached the last page. He looked at Oogie and Hahn, still not saying a word. He rose from his seat and walked around to their side of the table. He stood face-to-face with the two nervous designers.

'It has been many years since I have seen such impressive designs; you are both to be congratulated.'

Oogie and Hahn couldn't believe it.

'Let me explain what my company can do for you. We identify, prospect, contact buyers and manage the buying of your range.

'We also arrange appointments and constantly follow up with your customers. We have over 10,000 customer profiles on our books. We continually update and increase these profiles.

'We take a high profile during the Paris Fashion Weeks, and therefore, your outfits will be on shown to many buyers.'

'It sounds very impressive, Marc. Would you mind if Hahn and I discuss it overnight? We'll get back to you in the morning.'

'Not at all. I would expect you to talk it over.'

Hahn and Oogie thanked their host and caught a taxi back to the hotel.

'I don't feel like dining out, Oogie. Why don't we order room service.'

'I'm happy with that.'

Oogie ordered a steak sandwich while Hahn ordered a Caesar salad.

The meals arrived within thirty minutes.

'So, what are your thoughts about The Fashion Agent?' Oogie asked.

'I'm very impressed with their professionalism. I also believe they would ensure excellent exposure at the Fashion Weeks, but their commission is more than we are used to paying.'

'I agree with every point. However, I do believe if we wish to become a major brand in Paris we will need to pay a higher commission. It's not just Marc; it would be any Paris-based agency.'

'So you believe we should sign up with The Fashion Agent?'

'I do.'

'Okay, let's do it.'

Oogie called Marc the next morning, accepting his offer to represent the Oogie brand. Arrangements were made for the signing of the agreement that afternoon.

February 22 1983

Oogie and Hahn flew Singapore Airlines to Singapore the following day. They then boarded a Vietnam Airlines flight to Ho Chi Minh City.

A young man from the company met them and drove them back to Cao Lanh in the company's Land Rover.

As they entered the village, Hanh admired the development that had taken place since Oogie had first arrived.

Brick bungalows replaced the huts; a large diesel water pump had replaced the old motorbike water pump with underground pipes feeding both the village and the rice paddies. Several generators provided electricity to all the houses, communal hall, and the garment factory. Hanh's favourite project was the village school. It achieved several of the village's objectives. It educated the children and it also allowed the women to work in the garment factory and the men to work in the rice fields.

Hahn was keen to see her mother and father, as it had been over a year since she had seen them. She asked the driver to park outside her parents' bungalow. The couple entered the house of Hoa, her father, and Ngoc, her mother. They both greeted Hahn and Oogie with true warmth. There was much celebration the family was together at last… apart from Binh who had died in the Chinese war.

BUSINESS WITH THE DEVIL

CHAPTER 15

When Oogie and Hahn settled back in their routine they began to plan the expansion that would be required to service Australia and France. They calculated a further forty seamstresses were required. The neighbouring village of Cao Lanh would provide the majority of the new workforce. A second factory would need to be constructed in Cao Lanh to house the increased workforce. Overall, a significant investment would be required.

May 1 1983

Oogie made an appointment with the Vietin Bank in Ho Chi Minh City for the following Friday. The young fashion entrepreneurs had decided to borrow fifty percent of the capital required for the expansion. This would leave the company relatively liquid.

Oogie and Hahn were driven into the capital by the company driver, who dropped them outside the bank.

They were asked to wait in the manager's anteroom and they didn't have to wait long. A very distinguished man greeted them warmly. Mr Nguyen knew them both. Oogie's Fashions was regarded as a key account by the bank.

They explained the purpose of their visit and the amount required by the bank to achieve their expansion.

'I can't see why the bank would not advance the loan. If you complete this application while you're here, I'll submit it to the board. I would imagine we'll get back to you within a week.'

'Thank you, Mr Nguyen. We look forward to hearing from you,' said Oogie.

Mr Nguyen was true to his word; the bank approved the loan within the week. They could now begin the building project.

Hahn and Oogie decided to employ a construction company rather than project the build themselves as they did with the first one.

They appointed Universal Builders, a company of high reputation, to complete the project. It was expected to take six months to complete the project.

The build was 50% complete when a New York Department Store, Macy's, placed a significant order. Oogie Fashions had not approached the store. Macy's had placed the order based on Oogie's Fashion's reputation in Australia and Europe.

The only issue was that the second factory would not be complete within Macy's timetable.

Oogie and Hahn decided to travel to Hanoi where there were some excellent garment factories. Their objective was to contract a factory to complete the Macy's order.

They flew to Hanoi and checked into The Hotel Metropole Hanoi.

An appointment had been made before their departure with Northern Textiles, a large well-regarded garment factory.

The appointment time was for ten, the following day.

The young couple decided to eat in a street café rather than the hotel's dining room and they were not disappointed. The food was delicious.

The head office of Northern Textiles was located in central Hanoi, therefore Hahn and Oogie could walk rather than catch a taxi.

Once they arrived they were asked to wait in reception for Mr Chi, the Managing Director. He didn't keep them long before showing them into his large office.

'Can I offer you both a coffee?'

'No thank you, we have not long finished breakfast,' said Oogie.

'So, how can I help you?'

Hahn and Oogie explained they required a company, possibly Northern Textiles, to manufacture a large order of their designs.

Mr Chi agreed to quote on the order and get back to Hahn and Oogie within a week.

'Thank you, Mr Chi, we look forward to receiving your quote,' said Hahn.

'I look forward to doing business with Oogie Fashions. Can I arrange transport for you both?'

'No, that's not necessary. We're staying at the Hanoi Metropolitan Hotel, so we'll walk.'

As the young couple began walking to their hotel, Hahn sensed a feeling of anxiety from her husband.

'Is there something wrong, darling? I thought the meeting went very well.'

'It took me a while, but I finally worked out where I had met Chi before. He was the chief guard when I was imprisoned during the war. He was a cruel bastard. If I hadn't escaped, he would have tortured me to death.

'What I went through until I escaped was horrendous. Hahn, I'm not sure I could do business with this bastard.'

'I can understand your feelings, darling, but some good came out of your capture.'

'Like what?'

'If you hadn't been captured and then escaped you would never have met me. Look at the life we have created together.'

'You're right. That was the best thing that has ever happened to me, Hahn. Okay, I'll drop it, but I'll never forgive the bastard.'

Mr Chi submitted his quote for two thousand garments and Hahn and Oogie were impressed with the price. They notified Mr Chi that they accepted the quote and authorised him to begin production immediately.

September 1 1983

Three months later, Oogie flew to Hanoi to conduct a final quality control inspection before accepting the garments.

He checked into the Hanoi Hotel, placed his overnight bag in his room, and walked the one kilometre to Northern Textiles to meet with Mr Chi at the designated time of three o'clock.

He didn't have to wait long. Mr Chi greeted Oogie with a handshake and a smile.

'Good afternoon, Mr Chi.'

'Oogie please call me Sam.'

'Sam. That's an unusual Vietnamese name.'

'I travel overseas with this business. My real name is Duc which amuses many of my clients so I decided to change it.'

'I see what you mean.'

'Would you like to inspect some random garments, Oogie?'

'Yes, I would, thank you, Sam.'

Sam guided Oogie into a large warehouse where the Oogie Fashions garments were stacked at the entrance.

Oogie began examining the outfits meticulously. He ceased after he inspected forty garments.

'Sam, this workmanship is excellent. I congratulate you.'

'May I suggest we celebrate our new business relationship by having you join me for dinner?' suggested Sam.

Oogie was reluctant to accept but he remembered what Hahn had said.

'Yes thank you. I would be pleased to join you.'

'Excellent. I'll pick you up at your hotel at seven.'

The veteran Australian soldier walked back to the hotel with great trepidation. Memories flooded back of the beatings, the starvation, and the sheer feeling of helplessness.

Oogie caught the lift to the fifth storey room where he headed straight for the minibar and selected a Chivas Regal scotch. He added a few ice cubes and sat in the tub chair. He drank it slowly, contemplating if he would bring up his past with Sam. He had not made a decision when he opened the second bottle. Once he had finished the second mini bottle he still had not decided what to do.

Oogie showered and dressed in a white shirt and black pants. He went down to the foyer where he waited for his nemesis to arrive.

Oogie saw Sam pull up in a Toyota Land Cruiser. He waved to his new business partner. Oogie hopped in and Sam drove away.

'Where are we going Sam?'

'My favourite restaurant is La Badiane. It's not far from here.'

'It sounds French.'

'French Vietnamese actually.'

'Sounds good.'

Sam parked the car close to the restaurant. The two men walked the short distance to La Badiane where the owner, Mr Pham, greeted Sam like a brother. It was obvious Sam was a regular.

Mr Pham seated the two men at the best table in the house.

'Would you like to see a menu, Mr Sam?'

'No, just bring us your selections like you usually do.'

Twenty minutes later the entree arrived.

- Beef and noodle soup (pho bo)

Oogie enjoyed it very much.

The mains followed.

- Sizzling crepes (banh xeo)
- Sugar cane prawns

On the side

- Pickled vegetable salad
- Nuoc cham dipping sauce

These were followed by desserts.

- Banana coconut tapioca puddings (che chuoi)

Coffee

Oogie could not eat another thing. The meal was delicious.

'Would you care for a whisky before we go, Oogie?'

'I would like that.'

'Would Chivas Regal suit you?

'Absolutely! That's my favourite.'

Sam called the waiter over and ordered two doubles.

After they finished their drinks, Oogie found some Dutch courage.

'Sam, you may not realise, but we have met before.'

'I'm not aware of that, Oogie. Where exactly did we meet?'

'In the South Vietnam jungle. I was a POW and you were my captor.'

Sam looked horrified. He knew that meant he had been responsible for the capture and torture of his newfound business associate.

'Oogie, it was a horrible war. Both sides did terrible things to each other.'

'I don't think we treated our prisoners as badly as you did, Sam.'

'Oogie, the allies threaded wire through the hands of Viet Kong prisoners and threw them out of helicopters. There were over 400 civilians massacred at Mai Lai and there were many more massacres.

'We only wanted the unification of our country. You invaded our country.'

'Sam, I'll never forget what you and your men did to me and my comrades, but I'm prepared to let bygones be bygones.'

Both men raised their glasses.

'To peace.'

Sam paid the bill and drove Oogie back to his hotel. Once Oogie reached his room, he lay on the bed and became lost in his thoughts. He was pleased that he had confronted Sam but was also pleased they had reconciled.

He flew home the following day. When he saw Hahn, he expressed his pleasure with the quality of the work Northern Textiles had performed. He didn't mention his altercation and reconciliation with Sam.

A MOMENT IN MY ARMS, FOREVER IN MY HEART

CHAPTER 16

August 1984

Hahn and Oogie were sitting out on their veranda watching the Mekong river traffic. There were large barges, small fishing vessels and the odd patrol boat. Living on the river was one of the rewards they enjoyed due to their success.

'Oogie, are you happy?'

'Of course I am, darling. I'm married to you, we have a very successful business, good friends and we live in a beautiful house in a beautiful part of the world.'

'Yes, I agree, but there is something missing in our lives.'

'You mean children?'

'I do. We tried hard to conceive through IVF but to no avail. I desperately want to be a mother, Oogie. I think we should adopt a child.'

'Okay, we should approach a few orphanages in Ho Chi Minh City. I'd like to be a father. I think we would make good parents.'

Hahn approached a number of orphanages, and she and Oogie visited several. They decided to adopt a six-year-old boy from Dieu Giac Orphanage. His name was Tuan. His name meant bright and smart. They hoped he lived up to his name.

The day came when the expectant couple were due to take Tuan home to Cao Lanh and a new life.

Tuan became an orphan after both his parents died in a boating accident while they were net fishing on the Mekong.

The principal of the orphanage, Mrs Ngyen, led young Tuan out into the reception room where Hahn and Oogie waited with great anticipation.

'Tuan, these are Hahn and Oogie. They are your new parents. They are going to take you home to their beautiful village on the Mekong River. Isn't that exciting?'

'I don't want to leave my friends. I think I'd rather stay here.'

'Tuan, we will look after you and you can go to a very good school. There are many children in Cao Lanh, our village. I'm sure you will make many new friends,' said Hahn.

'What if I don't like it?'

'You can return here. It will be up to you.'

'Okay, I'll see how I go.'

Hahn and Oogie drove their new son back to the village.

Tuan was overwhelmed with the village. It was unlike anything he had seen before. When Oogie and Hahn arrived at their house he was amazed. He couldn't believe he had a bedroom to himself, for he was used to sleeping in a dormitory along with twenty other boys.

Tuan had only a rudimentary education at Dieu Giac, but he now attended the village school, reputed to be the best school in the south.

He excelled because he just wanted to learn.

After school, he worked in the garment factory two days a week, sweeping floors, and stacking garments. The other days he played soccer with the other boys in the village. He built a reputation as a fantastic striker. He also learned the importance of work and responsibility.

Tuan continued to excel at school. His favourite subjects were geography and history. That was not to say he didn't enjoy mathematics and science.

December 1990

'Hahn, do you agree we should take part in the Australian Fashion Week in Melbourne next year? said Oogie.

'I know it will be a great opportunity for us, but I'm just worried about leaving Tuan behind.'

'Can't we ask your parents to look after him? It will only be a couple of weeks,' said Oogie.

'Darling, they are getting old. Father turns eighty next month, and Mother is not far behind him.'

'Okay, let's think about it for a while.'

Oogie knew taking part in Fashion Week would improve their already strong sales in the Australian market.

Hahn said, 'Darling, I've been thinking about Mum and Dad taking care of Tuan. I'll ask them if they would feel comfortable doing so.'

'That's great Hahn, thank you.'

'Don't get too excited. They may say no.'

'I understand.'

The next morning Hahn approached her parents with the proposition of taking care of their grandson while she and Oogie travelled to Melbourne.

'Of course we would,' said her mother. 'We both love Tuan. It would be a wonderful experience.'

'Thank you both. I'm sure Tuan will enjoy living with you while we are away.'

The family always ate their evening meal together, and that included Hahn's parents. Hahn and Oogie decided to broach the subject after dinner.

'Tuan, Mummy and Daddy need to travel to Melbourne, Australia, in March next year for some very important business.'

Tuan looked alarmed. 'Who's going to look after me? I hope you are not sending me back to the orphanage.'

'No, darling. You are now our son. Ong and Ba (Grandma and Grandpa) are going to look after you.'

The boy looked relieved. 'Great I'd love that.'

'Excellent, so you're happy to stay home with Ba and Ong?'

'I sure am. I'm looking forward to it.'

Hahn and Oogie exchanged glances. They were relieved.

March 1 1991

Oogie and Hanh said their goodbyes. They would return in three weeks.

For now, Tuan would spend the time with his grandparents.

'Come on, Tuan, there is a special treat waiting for you,' said Hahn's mother.

'What is it?'

'Come inside and you'll see.'

They all entered the house and headed for the kitchen. Laid out on the table was a plate containing Banh Ba Nuang (Vietnamese Honeycomb Cake), which was Tuan's favourite.

Complementing the cake was Sinh To (Fruit Smoothie).

'Wow, that's looks delicious, Ba,' Tuan said.

The Snake

Trinh An, also known as con rắn, "The Snake", was Vietnam's most notorious gangster. Based in Ho Chi Minh City, he ran a criminal empire complete with gambling dens, hotels and restaurants that fronted brothels. The majority of the police force was on the gang's payroll; hence he and his gang members were rarely arrested.

An initiation was required for new members. The new recruit was required to plan a crime and execute it without mishap.

Vo Minh had grown up in the neighbouring village to Cao Lanh. He knew many of the kids in the village, having played soccer against them.

He had a deep ambition to become a gangster, and he knew he needed to devise a clever scheme if Trinh An was to accept him into the organisation.

Vo Minh was aware of Oogie and Hanh's wealth; everybody in the region was. He decided to kidnap Tuan and hold him for ransom. He thought US$100,000 would be an appropriate sum.

Vo Minh recruited three of his friends to take part in the crime, Cao Bao, Pham Huy and Dang Xuan.

'Vo Minh, do you anticipate the need for violence?' asked Pham Huy.

'I'm afraid we need to kill the boy's grandparents, because they know me.'

'Who's going to do the shooting?'

'I will.'

The family had just finished their treat when the front door was broken open. Four men all with AK47s forced their way in.

The leader appeared to be only a boy, a kid with a baby face.

He glared at Hanh's parents and shot them both with several rounds.

Tuan was in shock. His beloved grandparents lay bleeding on the kitchen floor. Two men manhandled Tuan into the Jeep and sped off down the dirt road.

Once outside the village, Vin Minh stopped the vehicle. He tied the boy's hands and feet and placed a blanket over him. He would remain in the back of the Jeep until they reached their destination.

Who were these men?

They were members of a criminal gang infamous throughout Vietnam.

THE SNAKE

CHAPTER 17

The Jeep sped through the jungle. The track had formed part of the Ho Chi Minh Trail. They were taking Tuan to an underground bunker in the Cu Chi tunnel system used during the war.

Cu Chi Tunnels

The tunnels of Củ Chi were an immense network of connecting tunnels located in the Củ Chi District of Ho Chi Minh City (Saigon), in Vietnam.

During the war, the Cu Chi tunnels were part of a much larger network of tunnels that underlaid much of the country. The Củ Chi tunnels were the location of several military campaigns during the Vietnam War and were the Viet Cong's base of operations for the Tết Offensive in 1968.

The tunnels were used by Viet Cong soldiers as hiding spots during combat, as well as serving as communication and supply routes, hospitals, food and weapon caches and living quarters for North Vietnamese fighters. The tunnel systems were of great importance to the Viet Cong in their resistance to American forces and helped to counter the growing American military effort.

American soldiers used the term "Black Echo" to describe the conditions within the tunnels. For the Viet Cong, life in the tunnels was difficult. Air, food, and water were scarce and the tunnels were infested with ants, venomous centipedes, snakes, scorpions, spiders, and rodents.

Most of the time, soldiers would spend the day in the tunnels working or resting and come out only at night to scavenge for supplies, tend their crops, or engage the enemy in battle. Sometimes, during periods of heavy bombing or American troop movement, they would be forced to remain underground for many days at a time. Sickness was rampant among the people living in the tunnels, especially malaria, which was the second-largest cause of death next to battle wounds.

Tuan's Cell

It was in these conditions that Tuan was kept in captivity.

March 1991

Several of the villagers approached the house when they saw the Jeep speed away. They had heard the shots and were concerned for the occupants' welfare.

The first person to enter the bungalow was Quan Gia, the village elder. He was horrified by what he discovered. He searched the house for Tuan but was unable to find him. He assumed the boy had been kidnapped. Oogie and Hahn had left their address in Australia in case they needed to be contacted. They left a phone number also. Quan Gia would need to travel to Ho Chi Minh City as there were no telecommunications in the village.

He instructed Oogie's driver to take him immediately. He was not looking forward to letting the couple know what had happened to Hahn's parents and about the disappearance of their son.

The trip took just over an hour and he instructed the driver to park near the post office.

Ho Chi Minh Post Office

It was here he could make an international telephone call. He hoped Oogie and Hanh would be in their hotel room. Quan Gia rang the Windsor Hotel. The operator rang the room. Oogie picked up the receiver after it had rung five times.

'Hello.'

'Oogie, it's Quan Gia.'

'Hello, is everything all right? Don't tell me the generator has broken down again.'

'No, but I have some very distressing news. Criminals shot dead Hahn's parents and they've taken the boy.'

'What! You must be mistaken. That can't be right.'

'I'm afraid so. I'm so sorry. I've got no idea where they've taken Tuan.'

'Quan Gia, don't notify the police. If you do, they will kill Tuan.'

Oogie placed the receiver down. He stared at Hahn.

'Darling what's wrong?'

'I'm afraid we have had some bad news, my love.'

'What?'

'Some gangsters broke into our house.'

'What did they take?'

'Tuan.'

'No.'

'I'm afraid so. They are holding him for ransom although there has not been a demand as yet.'

'Did they take my mother and father?'

'I don't know how to tell you this, Hahn… they killed them both.'

Hahn let out a bloodcurdling scream. 'NO.'

The telephone rang. It was reception, inquiring if everything was all right. A few guests had reported a possible murder.

'We received some very distressing news. We are both okay,' Oogie said.

'Is there anything we can do to help?'

'Yes, you can arrange for our bill. We need to check out tomorrow.'

Oogie contacted the airline to arrange flights to Vietnam the following day. He tried to console Hahn, but she was inconsolable.

He contacted Ross and explained what had happened. He asked if Ross could contact the management of Fashion Week and cancel Oogie Fashions' involvement. Ross was horrified by the news. He agreed to make the call.

The flight home was not a happy one. Neither Hahn or Oogie slept. They landed at Ho Chi Minh City airport, having endured the ten-hour flight.

Xuan, an employee, met them at the airport and drove them back to their village.

The one-hour trip was solemn. When they arrived at the village Quan Gia was waiting to greet them in the family house where the horrendous crime took place.

'Where can I view my parents, Quan Gia?' asked Hahn.

'We placed them in the cool room in the communal house.'

'I would like to see them.'

'Of course.'

The village elder led Hahn and Oogie to the communal house; the building Oogie had designed and helped build all those years ago.

At the far end of the house was a stainless steel cool room, which the grieving couple had donated to the people of the village.

Hahn and Oogie entered with trepidation. Lying on timber beds, covered with white shrouds, were Hahn's parents. The bodies had been covered in beautiful flowers.

Hahn kneeled beside them. Gently sobbing, she placed a flower on each parent, kissed their cheeks and left. Oogie followed her.

As they walked back to their home, Hahn asked Quan Gia when they could conduct the funeral.

'The funeral pyre is already built. You may have it whenever you wish.'

'I wish to have it tomorrow.'

'It will be so.'

The next day, the villagers assembled in front of the funeral altar. There was a statue of Buddha and incense sticks burning. The mourners placed flowers and fruit on the altar.

A monk blessed the deceased and then the pyre was set alight.

When Hahn and Oogie returned to their house after the funeral, both were thinking the same thing. Whoever perpetuated this hideous crime must be punished.

CAUGHT BETWEEN A ROCK AND A HARD PLACE

CHAPTER 18

After several hours driving, the Jeep pulled up beside a creek. The gangsters got out and lifted Tuan out. Dang Xuan undid the boy's blindfold and the strap around his ankles. The strap around his wrists remained.

The group entered the jungle, but after fifteen minutes they stopped.

Vo Minh brushed the leaves away from the jungle floor to disclose a trapdoor.

'Untie his hands,' Vo Minh instructed.

'I want you to climb down the ladder, Tuan. Don't be scared. I will follow you with a lamp.'

It was pitch black when the boy reached the bottom of the ladder. He looked up to see the light following him.

Each member of the gang also carried a lamp, so by the time all were in the cave they could see, albeit it was a pale light.

Vo Minh guided Tuan to a steel bed covered by a thin, dirty mattress.

'This is where you will sleep, boy. One of my men will bring you food and water twice a day. You shouldn't be here long. It depends on your parents.'

'What do you mean depends on my parents?'

'You must have realised by now you have been kidnapped. Your parents must pay a ransom to get you back.'

'What if they refuse?'

'You don't want to know.'

The men climbed the ladder and closed the trapdoor. Tuan was left in darkness apart from one hurricane lamp.

March 31 1991

2 am

The village of Cao Lanh was sleeping when a Jeep sped through the village. A rock was thrown through a window in Hahn and Oogie's house.

The couple sprang out of bed and discovered the rock on the kitchen floor. It was wrapped in the day's newspaper. Oogie unwrapped the paper, which contained the ransom note they were waiting for.

> *Con trai của bạn là an toàn cho bây giờ. Chúng tôi yêu cầu US $100000 cho trở lại của mình.*

> *Bạn sẽ cần phải làm theo một loạt các hướng dẫn. Việc đầu tiên là không liên lạc với cảnh sát.*

> *Chúng tôi sẽ liên lạc với bạn trong hai ngày với hướng dẫn them.*

> *Nếu bạn làm, chúng tôi sẽ cắt tai anh ấy*

'Your son is safe for now. We demand US$100,000 for his return.

'You will need to follow a series of instructions. The first; do not contact the police. If you do we will cut off his ears.

'We will contact you in two days with further instructions.'

'What do you think we should do? Obey their instructions or contact our friend Nguyen the Police Commissioner?' asked Hahn.

'You read what they threatened to do, Hahn. We can't afford to take the risk.'

'So, what do we do?'

'We wait for further instructions.'

Cu Chi Tunnel

April 1 1991

Tuan had been captive in the cave for what seemed like a year but was closer to a week. He could feel spiders crawl over his bare skin and heard what must have been a snake slither past him on more than one occasion.

Time went very slowly. He had nothing to occupy him other than his captors bringing him meals and water.

Two of Tuan's captors climbed down the ladder. It was unusual as it wasn't mealtime.

One of the men grabbed the young boy by his head while the other sliced off his right ear. Tuan screamed. They wrapped his head in a white bandage. They then left, taking Tuan's ear with them.

The severed ear accompanied the next ransom note, ensuring Oogie and Hahn how serious the kidnappers were.

Bạn phải đặt trong một túi đen US $ 100.000. Chiếc túi sẽ được đặt ở phía xa của Platform One tại Ga Trung tâm vào lúc 5 giờ chiều. Bạn phải bắt chuyến tàu 5 giờ chiều đến ga tiếp theo. Cậu bé sẽ đợi ở nhà ga. Anh ấy sẽ an toàn nếu bạn đã làm theo hướng dẫn của chúng tôi.

'On April 3rd, you are to place in a black bag US$100,000.

'The bag is to be placed at the far end of Platform One at Central Station at 5 pm exactly.

'You are to catch the next train to the following station.

'The boy will be waiting for you. He will remain safe if you have followed our instructions. Open the envelope. Its contents should convince you we are serious.'

'Oh my God, the bastards have cut off his ear!'

'If we ever catch these bastards it won't be their ears I cut off,' Oogie threatened. 'Can we raise US$100,000 this quickly?'

'We have to,' said Hahn.

'Okay, I'll go,' said Oogie.

'You're not going alone. I'm going with you.'

'We've only got two days to organise the money. We'd better get moving,' said Oogie.

'Don't worry; we'll raise it.'

April 2nd came and the parents were on tenterhooks all day. Their driver was ready to drive them to Ho Chi Minh City at 1 pm. They would be at the station in plenty of time.

The nervous parents arrived at Platform One fifteen minutes early. They placed the bag down at 5 pm exactly. They only had to wait five minutes for the train. They both felt extremely anxious. After a few minutes, the train pulled into the station. Oogie and Hahn stepped onto the platform. Tuan could not be seen. Their hearts sank, but Oogie spotted a large suitcase at the far end of the platform. They both ran down and Oogie gently lowered the case flat and opened it.

They both screamed.

Revenge

Xépôn is a village in Laos near the Vietnamese border. The village boasted an elementary school with three hundred students. There were six teachers, including Vu Ba Hoang who taught years five and six.

Xépôn School

Vu Ba Hoang returned home from another day at school. His wife, Chau, seemed pensive.

'What's the matter Chau?'

'I have some worrying news.'

'What is it?'

'I'm pregnant again.'

'That's wonderful, Chau! Why are you sad?'

'We are having trouble feeding our family as it is… how are we going to feed five?'

'Don't worry. I will find a way.'

After the family of four ate dinner, Vu Ba visited his good friend Quan Chinh.

'You look are little perturbed, my friend. Is there anything wrong?'

'Chau is pregnant again.'

'You should be happy. You never know; it might be a boy this time.'

'We are concerned that with an extra mouth to feed we won't have enough money to feed the family.'

'Oh, I see. I have a friend who approached me recently. He offered me a lot of money to take drugs over the border into Vietnam.'

'What do you call a lot of money?'

'A full year's pay for each trip made.'

'You mean to say each trip will be as much as I receive as a teacher for a full year?'

'Yes. So, what do you think?'

'I'd like to meet your friend.'

A meeting was arranged with Dang Chinh the drug dealer.

'It's simple, comrades, you take a backpack across the border where you will be met by one of our Vietnamese operatives. You hand over the bag and return to Xépôn. I will meet you and pay the money. I suggest you make six trips a year.'

'What if we get caught?'

'We have been operating for years. No one has been caught yet.'

'Okay, it sounds as if we should do it. When do you want us to start?'

'Next month.'

The two men did not mention their planned extracurricular activities. They felt their wives would worry.

Dang Chinh had lied about the length of time his organisation had operated the drug trafficking. This would be only the fifth operation.

Vo Minh was the organiser on behalf of the Snake, Trin An, and this was to be his first major operation since joining the gang.

At dawn on July 28, 1992, the two men, both carrying backpacks, trekked through a forest near the Vietnam-Laos border in Nghe An Province.

As the duo reached the forest's edge, they were ambushed by Vietnamese police officers.

Lieutenant Nguyen Dinh Tai grabbed Vu Ba Hoang by the arms and sent him sprawling onto the ground, where the police officer fired three bullets into the schoolteacher.

Remarkably, Vu Ba Hoang survived.

His colleague, Quan Chinh, was also shot but was able to return fire as he escaped into the jungle.

Vu Ba Hoang was arrested. Police found twenty packs of heroin weighing around 350 grams each, seven kilos of methamphetamine, and 12,000 pills of synthetic drugs in his backpack.

The schoolteacher was taken away and imprisoned until his trial date. The trial lasted less than a day before he was found guilty of drug smuggling and sentenced to death.

A week after his trial the father of three was executed by firing squad.

REVENGE

CHAPTER 19

August 15 1991

Life had changed for Oogie and Hahn. They both loved their adopted son Tuan and were devastated by his murder.

The couple threw themselves into their business as a way of coping with their tragic loss.

Oogie Fashions were now represented in Paris, London, Madrid, Rome plus Melbourne and Sydney. In America, they were represented in Los Angeles and New York.

Despite their business success and wealth, Hahn could not stop thinking about exacting revenge on the perpetrators of the heinous crime committed against their family.

Oogie and Hahn were sitting on their veranda enjoying a gin and tonic.

'Oogie do you ever think about revenge?'

'Of course, I do, darling, but what can we do?'

'Kill the bastards who mutilated our boy.'

'It's a great thought, my love, but how do we find these creeps?'

'Have you heard of General Vo Nguyen Giap?'

'Yes, he was head of the Vietnamese army.'

'He now has his own intelligence company. I think we should contact him and ask him to locate the gang members who kidnapped Tuan.'

'Do you think he would?'

'I do. He is very anti-drug smuggling. It is well known the gang is smuggling drugs from Laos to Vietnam.'

'Do you know how to contact him?'

'I do. Would you like me to arrange a meeting?'

'It wouldn't hurt.'

'I'll go ahead and arrange it.'

Hahn organised her driver to take her into Ho Chi Min City, where she checked into five star Mai House Hotel.

Mai House Hotel

She rang the number she was given by her Vietnamese warehouse manager who had reported to the general during the war.

'Hello, I would like to speak to General Vo Nguyen Giap please.'

'Who may I say is calling?'

'Hahn Jones of Oogie Fashions.'

'Wait while I see if the General is available to talk to you.'

Hahn waited for ten minutes. She began to think her call was futile.

'Hello, Hahn, this is Vo. How can I be of assistance?'

'I have a special request. May I suggest we meet at my hotel so that we can talk in private?'

'If it wasn't for your business reputation I would decline. However, I would be happy to meet you. What hotel?'

'Mai House. Would tomorrow afternoon at three suit you?'

'Yes, that would be fine.'

Hanh had organised for room service to deliver coffee and cakes to her suite.

Her telephone rang at 2.55 and reception announced General Vo Nguyen Giap wished to visit her suite. Hahn agreed; five minutes later the doorbell rang.

Hahn opened the door, admitting the General.

'Hello General, I'm pleased to meet you. Please take a seat. Can I offer you coffee?'

'Yes thank you.'

Hahn poured her guest a strong coffee. Sugar and milk?'

'Just milk thank you. Now, Hahn, what is it you wish to discuss with me?'

'Last March, a Saigon criminal gang kidnapped my son and held him captive. They cut off his ear to prove they were serious. They murdered my parents during the kidnapping.

'They demanded US$100,000 ransom, which we agreed to pay.

'We followed their instructions to the letter. We made the drop and followed their directions to collect our son.

'What we found was our beautiful boy dismembered and stuffed into a suitcase. I ask you to find these criminals so that I can deal with them.'

'I take it you will kill these beasts with your own hands?'

'I'd rather not say. I don't want you to be implicated.'

'Are you aware which gang was involved?'

'No, although I suspect it was the Snake.'

'I empathise with your situation. I charge $100 an hour and of course I have no idea how long it will take to identify and locate them. Do you agree to my terms?'

'I do. Money is not an issue. My husband and I will do anything to bring these bastards to justice.'

'Okay, we have an agreement. I will report back to you on a weekly basis.'

'Thank you, General, I have total faith in you. I know you will find these lowlifes.'

TO CATCH A SERPENT

CHAPTER 20

August 31 1991

Hahn returned to her village and briefed her husband on the results of her meeting with the General.

'What will we do when he locates these bastards?' asked Oogie.

'We take them out. As you know, I was a sniper during the war. I will have no trouble eliminating them.'

'Do you still have your rifle?'

'Yes, it's in the roof. However, the technology has improved significantly since the American war. I propose purchasing a high powered rifle on the black market.'

M82

The General was true to his word. He reported to Hahn and Oogie on a weekly basis. He had discovered that the gang was indeed the Snake, but he had not discovered what members had kidnapped and killed Tuan. Four weeks had passed when they received a new message from the General.

'Gặp tôi ở Nhà Mai vào ngày mai. Tôi có một số thông tin rất quan trọng cho bạn.

'Meet me at Mai House tomorrow at 12 noon. I have some very important information for you.'

Hahn and Oogie were excited. They knew the General would only summon them if he had discovered who these gangsters were and where they were located.

The expectant couple arrived at the hotel early. The General, accompanied by two of his men, entered the lobby on time.

'I am pleased to inform you that we have located the village where the four gangsters who murdered your son are located,' said the General. 'They are living in Xepon, which is located on the Vietnamese Laotian border. They base themselves there to receive drugs from Laotian drug mules.'

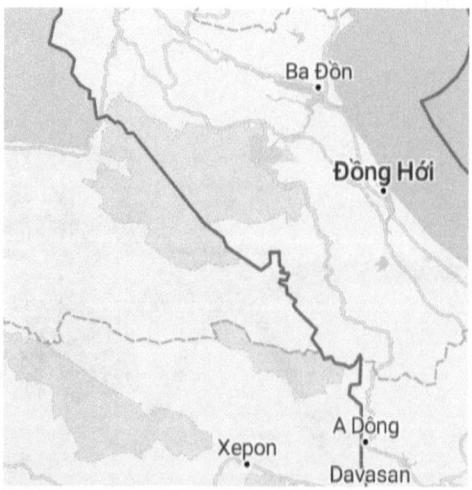

'I'm aware of Xepon. The Americans bombed it in an attempt to destroy the Ho Chi Min trail. They failed. It has a reasonable population, from memory.' Said Hahn.

'Yes, about 45,000.'

'Have you identified the houses they are occupying?'

'Yes, this is where we have been fortunate. All four are sharing the one house.'

'So we can hit them all at once?'

'You could, but I don't advise it. They live in a compound occupied by gang members. It would be dangerous to take them out in their bungalow.'

'What do you suggest?'

'Follow them into the jungle when they pick up the drugs. You will have plenty of natural camouflage and will be able to escape easily.'

'That sounds like a plan, but how will we know when they are leaving Xepon for a drug pick up?'

'I have had one of my men posted looking over the house; he will alert us. I suggest you rent a house near the compound. My people will help you secure a suitable residence.'

'Thank you, General; we are now close to avenging our son's murder.'

Hahn and Oogie moved into a small but comfortable house not far from the gang members. They felt comfortable that Trang Hai, their general manage, would take care of the fashion business during their absence.

Oogie was able to purchase a M82 sniper's rifle on the black market.

'I need to get some practice shooting, darling. Can we travel into a remote part of the jungle for some target practice?' asked Hahn.

'I would have thought all the jungle was remote.'

'You know what I mean.'

'When do you want to go?'

'What about tomorrow?'

'We can do that.'

They both rose early and ate a light breakfast. Oogie had hired a Land Cruiser the day before. The M82 had been loaded in a golf bag so as not to arouse suspicion. There was a golf course and resort fifty kilometres from Xepon.

Hahn had conducted some research and it was agreed they would drive eighty kilometres, park the car and walk into the jungle. Her reconnaissance indicated to her that there was a cleared patch about two acres in total one kilometre in. This would be a perfect location to place the target she had created the night before.

They found the cleared area and set up the target.

'I haven't shot a rifle in many years, let alone a rifle like this. I hope I can hit the target, if not the bull's eye.'

Hahn held the rifle, which was lighter than she expected.

This was a powerful carbine.

Range: 1000 metres

Calibre: .50 BMG

Rate of Fire: 200 rounds per minute

She held the butt against her shoulder and peered through the telescopic lens. She squeezed the trigger. The noise was significant, as was the recoil.

Her fears were realised when she missed the target altogether.

The ex-Viet Cong sniper raised the rifle again and slowly squeezed the trigger. This time she hit the edge of the target, hardly a marksman's shot.

'I've lost it.'

'Don't be silly, Hahn; you haven't fired a shot in many years. It's just like golf. If you haven't played in years it takes practice to get your game back.'

'I've never played golf.'

'I'm speaking metaphorically, darling. Now keep shooting. You'll get it back.'

Hahn continued to fire at the target. By the end of the day her accuracy had improved but she still had some way to go.

'We need to come back tomorrow.'

'Yes, I agree.'

They returned every day for the next seven days. By the end of the week, Hahn was hitting the bull's eye eighty percent of the time.

'I think you're ready, darling.'

'My aim was to hit the bull's eye a hundred percent of the time. That's what I used to do during the war.'

'You're not fighting in the war now, Hahn. These bastards' heads are a lot bigger than a bull's eye.'

'That's true.'

They returned to their house and waited to hear when the Snake gang were heading out to the jungle to receive the drugs from the Laotian mules.

They didn't have to wait long. The General's man knocked on their door the next day.

September 25 1991

'The gang is preparing to leave. I watched them load up their Toyota,' said Giang.

'Okay, thank you, we appreciate your diligence.'

'I'm going with you.'

'You don't have to. We'll be fine.'

'It's the General's orders. I'm to be your lookout.'

'Well then, welcome aboard,' said Oogie.

Oogie, Hahn and Giang waited in the Land Cruiser until they spotted the gang's vehicle departing the bungalow. They began to follow, ensuring they were not being observed.

The gang drove for two hours before taking a dirt road into the jungle. This was the most dangerous part of the journey. Oogie decided to stop at the edge of the jungle and take the punt that they would find the gang of four on foot.

His gamble paid off they only had to walk two kilometres. They sighted the four men sitting in a circle drinking whisky. They were obviously waiting for the drug mules.

The couple crept up to within about 500 metres from the group. Hahn placed the sniper's rifle on the tripod and lay flat on the ground.

She knew she had only one chance of taking the four gangsters out. If she missed, she and Oogie would be shot. The gang was heavily armed.

Hahn looked through the telescopic lens and fired the first shot. She didn't hesitate, but fired in rapid succession. It took thirty seconds for all four to die.

Giang picked up the M82 and they ran back to the Land Cruiser and sped away. There was a bridge over a large river ten kilometres on. Oogie stopped the vehicle halfway across and threw the rifle into the raging torrent.

They decided to remain in the rented house for another week so as not to arouse suspicion.

Oogie and Hahn returned home to Cao Lanh and their home, albeit it was a home without their son Tuan and Hahn's parents. Although they sadly missed their family members, they took some solace in knowing they had disposed of their killers.

'How do you feel about what we have just done, Hahn?'

'I feel very pleased. Those murderers deserved to die.'

'I agree. My conscience is clear.'

'What concerns me is the fact the Snake gang will continue with their evil ways. More innocents will be murdered, more drugs will be pushed and more young girls will be forced into prostitution.'

'I agree, but what can we do to stop them?'

'My understanding is the Shake comprises about one hundred gang members. What if we contacted General Vo Nguyen Giap and asked him if he would form a small army, say twenty soldiers? This military group would be responsible for eliminating the gang members.'

'Why do you think he would agree to that?'

'He is a businessman. We pay him for each soldier and additionally we pay him for each hit.'

'How much do you think we would have to pay him?'

'I don't know. We would have to work out what would be feasible.'

'Hahn, we need to determine a budget. If we decide we can afford it, then we can approach the General.'

'Let's think about it overnight and establish a proposal that we can put to the General.'

Hahn and Oogie retired for the night and in the morning over breakfast they discussed their ideas.

'I think we would have to pay an upfront fee for each soldier,' Hahn said.

'How much were you thinking?'

'US$5000.'

'That's a significant amount of money, darling.'

'Yes, it is but it's worth it and we can afford it.'

'Would there be any other costs?'

'There would be. I propose another US$5000 for each successful hit.'

'Hahn you're proposing a total cost of over US$5,000,000. Are you sure we can afford that sort of money?'

'That is one year's profit for the business. I'm sure we can sacrifice that amount.'

'You're the one who looks after the finances. If you say we can afford it then we can afford it.'

'We need to contact the General and arrange a meeting.'

'I'll call him this afternoon.'

Oogie called the General as agreed.

'Hello Oogie I didn't expect to hear from you so soon. What can I do for you?'

'Hello General, Hahn and I would like to meet with you. The sooner the better.'

'What's so urgent?'

'I can't discuss it over the phone, but I can tell you we have an extremely lucrative proposition we wish to put to you.'

'Now you have my attention. Would you be able to meet me in my office tomorrow? Let's make it 2pm.'

'Yes, that would be convenient.'

THE ELIMINATION

CHAPTER 21

October 5 1991

Oogie and Hahn arrived at the office tower where the General had his offices.

He was located on the eighth floor.

The receptionist asked them to take a seat, informing them the General would see them shortly.

After a fifteen-minute wait, the receptionist showed Oogie and Hahn into his office.

'Good morning, I didn't expect to see you both so soon. How can I help you?'

'Good morning, General. We have devised a plan in which we need your cooperation,' said Oogie.

The couple outlined their scheme.

'That's a very ambitious proposal. If I was to agree I would need to alter the payment schedule.'

'How so?' said Hahn.

'The amount you propose for each hit is generous, but you are assuming every member of the gang will be eliminated. I'm afraid there is no guarantee of achieving that.

'I would need to pay my men the majority of the fee, leaving my share much reduced.'

'What do you propose, General?'

'I would require an upfront fee of $50,000.'

Oogie and Hahn looked at each other.

'Would you mind if we took a little time to discuss it, General?'

'Not at all. Get back in touch when you have decided.'

'Oh, we just meant we'd go downstairs for a coffee. We shouldn't be more than an hour. We just need to rejig our budget.'

'That's fine. I'll see you when you get back.'

The husband and wife caught the lift down to the ground floor where the coffee shop was located.

They ordered two coffees and proceeded to sit at a table on the footpath in front of the coffee shop.

'What do you think Oogie?'

'We are proposing to spend over $5 million I don't think an extra $50,000 makes much difference. I can see his point. He needs to make a dollar if he takes this project on.'

'Yes, I see that. Finish your coffee and let's go back up and sign the deal.'

They returned to the General's office and asked to see him.

'That was quick. What's your decision?'

'We agree. Let's get started.'

'It will take some time to organise my men. As soon as the $50,000 hits my bank account I will get started.'

'Thank you, General, we will deposit the funds tomorrow.'

Oogie and Hahn returned home to their village where they arranged a transfer to the General's bank account the next morning.

Only a week had gone past when they received a handwritten note from the General.

Tôi vui mừng thông báo với bạn chúng tôi đã hạ gục thủ lĩnh của con rắn Trịnh Ân Các băng đảng đã bị suy yếu.

'I am pleased to inform you we have assassinated the leader of the Snake gang, Trinh An

'The gang has been weakened.'

Oogie and Hahn were delighted the evil bastard who created the Snake and directed its criminal activities had been taken out. The gang was now weakened and should now be an easier target.

Hahn dispatched $10,000 which included a $5,000 bonus for Trinh An.

The General's troops used various methods to despatch gang members.

It was common for gang members to share a house; usually four in all.

The General's men were nicknamed Mongoose for obvious reasons. They would throw grenades through the windows of the shared houses. This was a very efficient method of execution.

The most common method was the sniper's gun; a modus operandi familiar to Hahn's.

After a year, most of the Snake gang had been eliminated.

Oogie and Hahn decided to cease the operation, as the gang was now impotent and posed no real threat to the community.

The General disbanded his private army and the mongoose members were left to make their own way. The demand for private armies was limited. Some joined criminal gangs, and others laboured on farms.

One mongoose member, Quan, was particularly concerned as to how he could take care of his family. His wife and three children had grown accustomed to the lifestyle Quan could provide while working for the General. He joined a gang where he could utilise his military skills.

The gang had been the main rival to the Snake while it existed. Its name was Tiger. The gang leader was Binh; his name meant peaceful, and the irony wasn't lost on him.

Quan felt uneasy at first the Tiger gang was involved in drug smuggling, extortion and prostitution. They also provided hitman services for the right money.

Initially, the new recruit was involved in collecting money from businesses involved in the extortion racket. Eventually, Binh decided to utilise Quan's military skills. A rival gang member had been caught infringing on the Tiger's drug business. There was only one thing to do, exterminate him.

'Quan, the boss wants to see you in his office,' said Chinh.

'Shit, do you know why? I haven't done anything wrong.'

'No, I'm sure you'll be okay. You'd better get a move on. He doesn't like to be kept waiting.'

'Wish me luck. I think I'm going to need it.'

Quan walked slowly to Binh's office. He had been in it only once before when Binh hired him.

He knocked on the large teak door.

'Come in.'

Quan entered the dark office, his head bowed.

'Sit down, Quan. I have a job for you.'

'Yes, Boss.'

'I want you to take out a fellow called Sinh. He has stolen a significant amount of heroin from us. With your background, it should be a piece of cake.'

'When you say take out, what do you exactly mean?'

'I mean execute the bastard, Quan. There will be a bonus for you when you complete the job.'

'Where do I find this person, Boss?'

'All the details of his favourite haunts and his home address are in this envelope along with a photo so you can recognise him. I suggest you take him out in a public place rather than his home. Here, take this Glock. Make sure you dispose of it after you shoot the bastard.'

Glock Hand Gun

'When do you want me to hit him?'

'As soon as you can.'

As Quan left Binh's office, he felt a great deal of trepidation. He knew it was essential that he completed the job successfully. His future depended on it.

The following day, he visited Sinh's favourite café. He couldn't believe his luck. His target was sitting at a table on the footpath.

Quan walked calmly up to Sinh's table, pulled out his pistol and put three bullets into his head. He then walked quickly down the street and into a laneway. The other patrons took no notice. They were more concerned with the man bleeding on the footpath.

There was one patron who did see the shooting. He was a senior policeman, a Sergeant in the Homicide Squad. One of Trang's abilities was being able to remember a face. He not only remembered Quan's face; he recognised it. Trang was involved in the Snake killings.

Quan was in custody twenty-four hours after the shooting.

The assassin was in a cell with about thirty other suspects waiting to be questioned. His name was called. He approached the barred gate, where he was handcuffed and led out to an interrogation room.

Sergeant Trang was sitting at a desk ready to begin the questioning.

Quan was sat down opposite the policeman and was handcuffed to the desk.

'My name is Sergeant Trang and I believe you are Quan. Is that correct?'

'You know it is.'

'We don't like gang wars in Vietnam. We believe you were part of the gang that wiped out the Snake gang. Can you tell me who headed up the gang?'

'I don't know what you're talking about.'

'If you are convicted of that poor man's murder, you will spend the rest of your life in gaol. How do you think your wife and children will cope without you?'

'That poor man was a heroin dealer.'

'Look, here's the deal. You divulge who the leader of the gang was and I'll get you out of here scot-free.'

'Let me think about it.'

'I wouldn't think too long. I might change my mind.'

'When do you want an answer?'

'Tomorrow at the latest.'

'How do I know you'll keep your side of the bargain?'

'Trust me. I'm a man of my word.'

'His name is General Vo Nguyen Giap.'

'I don't believe you. I know him he is a man of integrity.'

'You asked me and I've told you. I should be able to get another member of the group to verify what I've told you.'

'Can you get hold of him quickly?'

'Get me a telephone and I'll call him. He is a good friend. He'll come.'

The telephone call was made and Quan's friend and colleague Trung agreed to come to the police station.

Trung verified that the General led the group that massacred the Snake gang.

October 12 1991

Sergeant Trang decided he needed to inform the Police Commissioner, Mien Tran. He called the Commissioner's PA and requested a meeting.

She confirmed an appointment for 10 am the following day.

Sergeant Trang arrived fifteen minutes early, as he knew the Commissioner frowned on his staff being late.

'Sergeant Trang, the Commissioner will see you now.'

The policeman had only met his chief face-to-face once before when Trang had received a medal for bravery.

'Good morning, Sergeant, how may I help you?'

'Sir, we have discovered who led the group that destroyed the Snake gang.'

'That's excellent, who was it?'

'General Vo Nguyen Giap.'

'Well done. Has he been arrested yet?'

'Not, yet sir, we thought we should wait until we informed you.'

'Yes, good thinking. Why don't you hold off until I can write a press release.'

'Yes, sir.'

'You're dismissed. Good work Sergeant.'

When the Sergeant left the office, the Commissioner sat down at his mahogany desk.

The General was one of his best friends. They had been in the Vietnamese Intelligence Department together during the war. He couldn't allow his great friend to be incarcerated.

October 14 1991

The General picked up his private telephone.

'Hello, this is General Vo Nguyen Giap.'

'Pham, it's Mien. You are in great danger.'

'How so, Mien Tran?'

'My department has discovered it was you that eliminated the Snake gang. Your arrest is imminent. You need to flee Vietnam immediately.'

'I thought the police would be glad to see the last of those murderous bastards.'

'True, we were, but you can't murder eighty people at your discretion.'

'Okay, I'll take your advice. I'll leave tonight.'

'Where do you intend to go?'

'Best you don't know. I'll let you know later when I know I'm safe.'

'Good luck, my friend.'

'Thank you for the warning, Mien.'

The General knew he had to warn Oogie and Hahn as it was inevitable the police would discover their involvement in the gang war.

He called the Oogie Fashions office and Hahn answered the phone.

'Hahn, the police know about my involvement in the Snake slaughter. I'm fleeing the country. I suggest you and Oogie do the same. If you decide to stay in Vietnam you could spend the rest of your lives in prison.'

'Do you really think so?'

'I know so. Leave as soon as you can.'

The General was a very wealthy man and he knew he had to transfer his funds to a Thailand bank as soon as possible.

He transferred $US10, 000,000 to the Bangkok Bank; the largest bank in Thailand.

October 16 1991

He and his wife and two children flew out the same night.

Hahn informed Oogie of the telephone conversation.

'So, do you think we should go?'

'Well, let me see… spend the rest of our lives in prison or fly out to Melbourne. I think we should choose Melbourne.'

'What about our business?'

'Well, if you think about it, most of our revenue is generated offshore. Trang Hai can continue running our manufacturing in Vietnam. If things get too hot, we can move our manufacturing to somewhere like Bangladesh.

'Hanh, you need to book two business class tickets to Melbourne immediately.'

The couple booked business class seats on Singapore Airlines. They departed on October 17 1991.

SILENCE IS GOLDEN

CHAPTER 22

November 1992

General Vo Nguyen Giap was able to find a luxury apartment near Sukhumvit Road in central Bangkok. He and his family were very comfortable. The General had established a security firm and his children attended the American School.

Vo was sitting in his favourite chair overlooking the Bangkok skyline, reading Time Magazine.

When his phone rang, he was annoyed at being disturbed as he was reading about Bill Clinton who had been recently elected President of the United States.

'Hello Vo, it's Mien. How are you?'

'I'm fine, my old friend. All the better from hearing your voice.'

'I'm planning on visiting Bangkok. I was hoping we could catch up?'

'Of cause we can. Why don't you stay with us? There is plenty of room.'

'I don't think that would be a good idea.'

'No, I suppose you are right.'

'I've booked a suite at the Intercontinental. It's close to your apartment.'

'When are you planning on arriving, Mien?'

'Next Monday. I've booked a conference room.'

'That sounds very formal. It's not a social visit I take it?'

'I'm looking forward to seeing you, my old friend, but I wish to discuss a business proposition with you.'

'Now you have my interest, Mien. I look forward to seeing you next Monday.'

The General was intrigued. He'd departed Vietnam under a cloud and if he returned he would be arrested and probably executed, yet the country's Police Commissioner had a business proposition he wished to put to him. Next Monday couldn't quickly enough.

November 15 1992

The Vietnamese Police Commissioner landed at Suvarnabhumi Airport, Bangkok at 10 am. He caught a taxi to the Intercontinental Hotel where he was due to meet his friend Vo at noon.

General Nguyen Giap asked reception to notify his friend of his arrival.

The receptionist called the Presidential Suite.

'Hello, sir, a gentleman is requesting your room number.'

'What's his name?'

'General Nguyen Giap.'

'I'm expecting him. Please send him up.'

The General caught the lift to the 30th floor. He rang the bell of the Presidential Suite. Mien hugged his friend and invited him into the magnificent suite.

'Can I order you some coffee, Vo?'

'Did you say you booked a conference room? Why don't we get our coffee delivered to the conference room.'

'I did, but when I discovered they allocated me the Presidential Suite I cancelled it. The suite has its own conference room.'

'Okay then, yes, I would love a coffee.'

'So, while we wait for room service we could begin our discussion.'

'I am very keen to hear your proposal.'

'Vo, I know you despise the heroin traffic as much as I do.'

'I certainly do. After all, that's why I am an exile.'

'You would be aware that the Golden Triangle covers Thailand, Burma and Laos; 950,000 square kilometres in all.

'Burma is the largest producer of opium in the world. It has 430 square kilometres under cultivation.

'The Burmese government lacks any real commitment against the cultivation and sale of opium.

'The Thai government has tried unsuccessfully to reduce the poppy crops and Laos is indifferent.'

'Mien, what's this got to me?'

'I am part of a consortium that is committed to eradicating the poppy trade in the Golden Triangle.'

'With due respect, the governments of the three countries involved have had little success, so how do you expect a private consortium to succeed?'

'The consortium is large, comprising some of the richest people in the world. They are all committed to eradicating the heroin trade. The consortium members in the past have contributed to the eradication of polio, malaria, and HIV to name a few. They see heroin as a major health hazard that must be eradicated.'

'So what is the budget for the heroin eradication program?'

'US$100,000,000 to begin with.'

'My God, they are serious, aren't they?'

'Yes, my friend, over 600,000 people die from a heroin overdose each year. Add that to the lives ruined and it truly is a pandemic.'

'So where do I fit into this plan?'

'We want you to manage the operation. You are the most experienced military person I know.'

'I hate to bring it up, but how much do you propose to pay me?'

'A significant part of your fee will be success-based; however a base payment of US$500,000 will be paid on your appointment.'

'That's very generous. What resources have you been able to recruit?'

'We have 220 mercenaries, ex-soldiers, all vetted and all trained. We also have eighteen Huey helicopters, all with experienced pilots.'

'Are the choppers to ferry in the troops?'

'Yes, partly, but their main purpose is to drop napalm bombs on the poppy fields.'

'Wouldn't that put the villagers at risk?'

'Normally yes, but we intend to attack at night. The villagers will all be asleep in their beds. All the pilots are experienced at flying at night. So, are you in, Vo?'

'Yes, Mien, you can count me in. When do we start?'

'We need to hit them just before harvest time. Therefore early July would be ideal.'

'That's more than six months away.'

'I assure you, Vo, we will need the time for planning and training. This operation is complex.'

'I suppose you're right. I should know from my experience. Do we have a name for this operation?'

'PEPA. It is an anagram for Poppy Eradication Program Asia.'

'That's a catchy name.'

'Yes, I thought so.'

'Where do you propose to locate PEPA's base?'

'Fifty kilometres outside of Chaing Rai. It is strategically located in Northern Thailand yet close to the poppy fields of Burma and Laos.'

'Is the base already constructed?'

'Yes, we cleared the jungle and built the base last year.'

'Were the local villages suspicious?'

'There are no local villagers. It's deep in the jungle.'

'When do you require me to travel up north?'

'We won't need you on location for a little while. In the meantime, you can direct the operation from Bangkok.'

'When should I expect my retainer?'

'It should be in your bank in the next few days.'

'Well, Mien, I look forward to working with you.'

'As I do with you, my friend.'

LET THE POPPY WAR BEGIN

CHAPTER 23

When the General returned to Bangkok, he informed his wife Mai that he had been appointed project manager for a dam construction project in northern Thailand. It would require time away from the family, but the contract was lucrative.

Although not happy about his impending absence, she was pleased her husband would once again be earning good money.

Two days after his arrival back in Bangkok, US$500,000 was deposited in Vo's bank account.

There were many things to organise despite the base being completed. He needed to arrange his army of mercenaries to be clandestinely transported to the base. More difficult was the transport of the helicopters. They needed to fly to the Chaing Rai region without attracting attention. This would require flying separately a few days apart, and at night.

One of the 18 Huey Helicopters Used in PEPA

Trucks would be required to transport weapons, including napalm bombs hidden under bags of rice.

The rice would be used by the mercenaries as well as foodstuffs required by the troops. One thousand bottles of water were also shipped up to the PEPA camp. The General was experienced in the logistics of war.

The General's troops were required to run ten kilometres a day along the jungle tracks. It was essential that the men maintained a high level of fitness.

On the 30th of June, two significant events occurred. The General received the go-ahead to begin the operation.

Hahn received unexpected news.

Melbourne June 30

When Oogie arrived home from his meeting with Myers, he was pleased with the result. The major store had agreed to increase its Oogie Fashions orders by 25% over the summer.

He reported this to his wife.

'That is good news darling,' Hahn agreed. 'It might inspire David Jones to follow suit. I have some great news also. I'm pregnant.'

'No, you can't be. I mean, how?'

'Surely you would know how.'

'You know what I mean. We were told you couldn't conceive.'

'Well apparently I can and I did.'

'This is wonderful news, my love. I can't believe it.'

The couple hugged each other and kissed.

'When we lost Tuan I thought it was our last chance to raise a family. This is the best news I've ever received,' said Oogie.

'The baby is due in February.'

'Darling, we need to celebrate. Let's invite Rosco and Loretta over for dinner this Saturday night.'

'Yes, why not. You can call them.'

Oogie made the call. He had intended not to break the news to his old friend until Saturday night. However, he couldn't help himself.

'Hahn and I have some exciting news; she's pregnant. All these years we were told she couldn't conceive then out of the blue...'

'Mate! That's fantastic news.'

'Hanh and I would love to have you and Loretta over for dinner this Saturday night to help us celebrate.'

'We are meant to be going to Government House for a charity dinner, but we'll drop that and head to your place to help you celebrate.'

'Are you sure? It sounds like an important dinner.'

'It's not as important as your dinner, mate. We will donate a significant amount to the cause, as we always do.'

'Can you make it 7 pm?'

'We'll be there. I have been holding onto a special bottle of champagne. This is the occasion I've been waiting for to crack it.'

Oogie and Hahn's Hawthorne House

The doorbell rang at 7 pm, and Oogie opened the door, giving both Ross and Loretta a hug. They moved into the kitchen where Hahn was preparing the meal. The hugging ceremony was repeated.

Rosco handed over the 1971 Dom Perignon.

'It's still cold. Why don't you open it and pour us all a glass.'

'What a wonderful idea.'

Once all four glasses were filled, a toast was made.

'Here's to Hahn and Oogie. Congratulations and may you both enjoy this wonderful new life as parents together.'

The two couples had a wonderful night. Hahn had prepared a Vietnamese feast. Oogie provided some excellent Australian wine.

Chiang Rai Vietnam

At the same time Oogie and Hanh were hosting their dinner in Melbourne, General Vo Nguyen Giap was finalising the poppy raids.

Eighteen Huey choppers with twelve highly trained mercenaries aboard each helicopter took off for the poppy fields of Burma. The Hueys had a full complement of barrel bombs containing napalm.

The weapons on the PEPA helicopters included auto-cannons, machine guns and rockets. The Hueys also carried air-to-surface missiles to be used as a self-defence weapon.

The plan was to land the choppers and take out the drug lords' troops. The choppers would then drop the napalm, burning as much of the plantation as they could. The remaining untouched poppy fields would be destroyed the next night. The plan was to raid the plantations until they were largely destroyed.

The PEPA helicopters with all soldiers accounted for returned to the base from Burma at 2 am.

Aerial photos verified 10,000 hectares of poppy fields had been destroyed. The objective was 50,000 hectares, so there was more work to be done. Once they completed the Burma raids they would move on to Laos and finally Thailand.

The General knew it was the element of surprise that ensured the success of the initial raids. He also knew that the enemy would be well prepared for further attacks. There was no doubt the drug lords would strengthen their defences.

The PEPA consortium decided to hold off any further raids, hoping that the drug lords would become complacent.

The second series of raids took place four weeks after the first. The results were similar to the initial attack, but two Huey helicopters were shot down by Russian surface-to-air missiles with a loss of twenty PEPA troops. The PEPA choppers' air-to-surface missiles were ineffective against the superior Russian weapons.

August 21

Although the consortium of philanthropists was happy that half the poppy fields had been destroyed, they were devastated with the number of casualties. The General was summoned to San Francisco to brief the consortium on the success of the project and the projected results for future operations.

He flew business class. He had a room booked at the Ritz Carlton. A conference room in the same hotel had also been booked.

The day after his arrival, at 10 am, Vo walked into the conference room. Sitting around the boardroom were eight highly distinctive billionaires. The General had not met any of them before but he recognised all of them.

'Welcome to San Francisco, General,' said the man at the end of the table.

'Thank you, sir.'

'Please call me Bill.'

'Thank you, Bill. Please call me Vo.'

Introductions continued.

'Now we have the niceties out of the way maybe we can discuss the PEPA project,' said the one called Jeff.

'All right, Jeff. Vo, can we have your report relating to the PEPA project please?' asked Bill.

'The first two attacks on the Burma poppy fields destroyed 20,000 hectares. Therefore 30,000 remain; a sizeable amount but I believe within our capability.

'As you are all aware, we suffered twenty casualties during the second raid; a tragedy, but we are fighting a war.'

'Were you expecting such heavy casualties, General?' asked Warren.

'In a war it is impossible to model how many casualties will occur. We were aware that the enemy i.e. the drug lords, would be heavily armed. We did underestimate the weaponry at their disposal.'

'When you say you underestimated their weaponry, which weapons do you refer to?' asked Larry.

'The Russian surface-to-air missiles that brought down the two choppers and killed twenty of our finest.'

'How can we avoid such carnage in the future, General?'

'The troops we have are the finest soldiers available, mainly SAS from Britain, Australia and the USA. The assault rifles used are the Russian Kalasnikov.'

'Why are we using Russian AK47s?' asked Larry.

'Because they are the best assault rifle available in the world.'

'I know they were comparatively cheap but are you confident the Huey helicopters are the right chopper for the job?' asked Warren.

'The Huey was the most successful troop carrier and gun ship in the Vietnam War. I cannot think of a better helicopter to use in our PEPA program.'

'So how do we minimise our casualties?

'If we purchase the right weapons we should be able to achieve our objectives.'

'General, you have extolled the virtues of the AK47 rifle and the Huey helicopter. Now you are suggesting they are not suitable. I am confused,' said Sergey.

'I am not denigrating our existing weaponry; I am suggesting additional high grade weapons.'

'What exactly are you suggesting?'

'Two MiG 27s; fully optioned.'

MiG 27

'Are we talking white wall tiles?'

'No. I mean 1 × 30 mm Gryazev-Shipunov GSh-6-30 rotary cannon with 260 rounds. 1 × 23 mm Gryazev-Shipunov GSh-23 autocannon with 200 rounds. Napalm bombs.'

MiG 27 Fully Optioned

'What sort of investment are we talking about? We all have deep pockets but there is a limit.'

'We can lease the aircraft together with two fighter pilots for US$2,000,000 a month.'

'Where will we source them?'

'I'm not sure where they are sourced from, but I suspect North Korea. I have had dealings with a Saudi arms dealer; Ahmad Aman. He assures me the planes can be leased. He could source a destroyer if you wanted one.'

'I don't think we would need a destroyer in the Burmese jungle,' said Michael.

'I take it insurance would be difficult to obtain for a MiG 27?' asked Larry.

'Yes, I'm afraid to say if we lose a fighter we are up for the replacement cost.'

'How much would we be up for?' Bill asked.

'A second hand MiG 27 sells for about US$5,000,000.'

'That's not too bad. What about the pilot?'

'If in fact it's North Korea, the government would take care of his family.'

'Run through the plan of attack, General,' said Warren.

'The initial phase will encompass the Hueys bringing in our troops. They would attack the drug lords' troops. The MiG 27s would take out the surface to air missiles using sophisticated radar.

'The MiGs would strafe the barracks, ensuring the enemy was destroyed.

'The Hueys and the MiGs would then drop the napalm bombs.

'I believe it will be mission accomplished. We then move on to Laos.'

'General, you seem confident this plan of attack will be successful. Can we ask you to come back at the same time tomorrow? In the meantime, we will discuss whether we finance your proposal,' said Bill.

'Certainly. If you require further information you know where to contact me.'

Vo returned to his suite and telephoned his wife, informing her of his delayed return.

He ordered room service and watched his favourite TV show, *Sex and the City*. He retired at 10 pm and rose at 6 am. He decided to eat breakfast in the dining room.

General Vo Nguyen Giap entered the conference room at 10 am to find all eight consortium members seated at the conference table.

'General, we have discussed your proposed plan of attack and although we did not reach a unanimous decision, a majority voted in favour,' said Bill.

'I'm sure you all will be pleased with the result. The sooner we rid the world of this scourge the better.'

'We appreciate your commitment, General. May we suggest you arrange the planes ASAP? We will deposit the funds in the PEPA account as usual. I know we leave the logistics up to you but we were wondering what airport you intend to use?' asked Mark.

'Chiang Rai. The Thai Government have given us permission albeit secretly.'

'That's excellent, thank you, General. I bring this meeting to a close,' said Bill.

All the consortium members dispersed, returning to their home states and countries.

General Vo flew back to Bangkok to begin the planning process.

He contacted Ahmad Aman, giving him the go-ahead for the two MiG 27s.

The fighter jets and their pilots were ready to attack from Chiang Ra airport by 30th September.

The date chosen for the final attack in Burma was 15 October.

Sixteen helicopters carrying twelve SAS troops flew into the remaining fields, using cannon to blast the barracks of the soldiers. The MiG 27s then strafed the barracks to ensure all occupants had been eliminated. The next task was to identify the surface-to-air missiles using sophisticated radar. The MiGs then destroyed the missile batteries. The

MiGs and the helicopters were able to bomb the poppy fields using napalm bombs.

By the end of the night, 80% of the remaining poppy fields had been destroyed; 24000 hectares in all. The mercenaries destroyed the remaining 6000 hectares the following night without casualties.

The same modus operandi, using the same equipment, was adopted in Laos and Thailand. PEPA was just as successful in both countries, but there were casualties, fifteen in all.

The PEPA consortium accepted the loss reluctantly. They committed to a payment of US$1,000,000 to each soldier's next of kin.

GOLDEN TRIANGLE

DESTROYED

LIGHT MY FIRE

CHAPTER 24

February 1995 Vietnam

Danh was a long-term employee at Oogie Fashions. He was not known for his intellect, but he was known for his honesty and diligence. He was a security guard at the company's warehouse.

Danh lived in a cottage on the warehouse grounds. This situation was convenient for both parties.

February 17 1995

Danh's favourite alcoholic drink was whisky… nothing too expensive, as it had to meet his budget. His whisky of choice was Dewar's.

On the night of February 17, he consumed more than he should have. He fell asleep at 8 pm and stayed asleep until 1 am. What woke him from his drunken slumber was the smell of acrid smoke. Danh reluctantly got out of bed and looked out the window. What he saw horrified him. The warehouse was well alight. The fire brigade was attempting to douse the flames. Someone had called them. Obviously not him.

Danh remained awake for the remainder of the night desperately hoping the warehouse could be saved. When the sun rose, it became clear the warehouse and all its contents had been destroyed.

Giang, the warehouse manager, was devastated. How could this happen?'

He needed to telephone Hahn and Oogie and inform them of the tragedy.

Melbourne Australia

Hahn had just prepared a chicken stir-fry. Ivy, her four-year-old daughter, loved this dish.

Hanh was waiting for Oogie to arrive home from the office. Their regime was to enjoy a glass of wine before dinner.

When the telephone rang, Hanh answered it.

'Hello Hahn, it's Giang.'

'Hello Giang, how are you?'

'Not so good. Is Oogie home?'

'No, he's not home from work yet although I'm expecting him at any moment.'

'May I ask you to call me when he gets home? I need to talk to both of you.'

'Giang, is there something wrong? You're not resigning, are you?'

'No, not unless you want me to.'

'Don't be silly, we'll call you when he gets home.'

Hanh had just put down the receiver when Oogie walked in. She explained the strange telephone call to her husband.

'Well, we'd better call him.'

Oogie telephoned his warehouse manager.

'Hello Giang, is there a problem?'

'I'm afraid there is, Oogie. There was a fire at the warehouse last night.'

'Bugger, was there much damage?'

'The warehouse and all the garments have been completely destroyed.'

'Was anybody injured?'

'No, there was nobody in the building at the time.'

'Okay, Giang I'll let you know what our plans will be.'

'Goodbye Oogie.'

'We'll speak soon. Bye.'

'What are we going to do, darling? All the garments in the warehouse were ready to ship out to our outlets,' said Hahn.

'I need to fly out to Vietnam with the patterns. I'll contact Mr Chi at Northern Textiles. They proved to be reliable before despite Chi being my nemesis. I'll go as soon as I can arrange a flight.'

Oogie was able to fly out the following night. His intended to stay a week.

Oogie kissed his wife and daughter goodbye, then took a taxi to Melbourne Airport to catch the Vietnam Airlines plane to Ho Chi Minh City.

He settled into the business class seat and waited for the announcement to take off.

The plane powered down the runway and slowly lifted into the sky. The flight attendant offered Oogie a drink. He chose whisky and she returned with a Chivas Regal.

They were four hours into the journey when the passengers heard a loud bang. The Captain made no announcement, so the passengers discounted the noise. If there were a problem, the Captain would have announced the fact.

Half an hour later, another bang reverberated through the cabin. This time, the Captain announced that both engines had exploded. He instructed the passengers and flight crew to be seated. He intended to crash land in the South China Sea.

Oogie looked at the woman sitting next to him. 'We're not going to make this.'

The Captain and co-pilot struggled to bring the plane in on a steady course, but unfortunately the airline hit the water at speed and sank almost immediately. All passengers and crew died.

Canberra ACT Australia

The Prime Minister of Australia, Graham Hodges, was in his office discussing drought relief with his Agriculture Minister, Frank

Worthington. His Chief of Staff rang, asking to interrupt the meeting with some important news.

'Mr Prime Minister, a Vietnamese Airlines airliner has gone missing en route from Melbourne to Ho Chi Min City.'

'That's terrible! How many Australians were on board?'

'It is believed 230 of the 250 passengers were Australians.'

'Oh, my God. Do we know where it went down?'

'We have some idea but we can't be sure.'

'We need to commit the appropriate resources to find this aircraft. Please call the Vietnamese President. This needs to be a joint search.'

At around the same time the Prime Minister was informed, Hahn was notified by the Australian Department of Foreign Affairs.

She was devastated. Her only hope was that Oogie had survived the crash.

The disappearance on 25 February 1995 of Vietnam Airlines Flight 333, a scheduled flight from Melbourne International Airport to Ho Chi Minh City, prompted a significant search in the South China Sea. This became one of the most expensive search operations, surpassed only by the search for Malaysia Airlines 370.

Analysis of the flight path enabled both planes and naval destroyers to search the most probable crash sites. After a month's search, the operation was abandoned.

Searching for Vietnamese Airlines 333

THE DEVIL WEARS ZARA

CHAPTER 25

Hahn had now accepted that Oogie was lost. The love of her life and her business partner was gone.

A memorial service was held at Saint Paul's Cathedral in Melbourne. Eleven hundred people attended, including the Premier of Victoria, the Lord Mayor and various business leaders.

Ross gave the eulogy, which brought many of the congregation to tears.

Soon after the funeral, Ross and Loretta invited Hahn and Ivy over for dinner.

The taxi parked in front of the Toorak home's entrance.

Hahn rang the doorbell and the door opened almost immediately.

Ross hugged his good friend, then picked up Ivy and gave her a kiss. Loretta joined them, also hugging Hahn and Ivy.

'Come on in you two; it's starting to rain,' said Loretta. 'Can I get you a drink, Hahn? What about you, Ivy? Would you like an orange juice?'

Over dinner, Ross broached the sensitive subject.

'Hahn, have you decided whether you will continue on with the business?'

'I'm not sure, Ross. Running Oogie Fashions without Oogie seems incongruous.'

'Yes, I know what you mean. Would you consider selling the business?'

'I would for the right price. If I could sell I could dedicate more time to Ivy.'

'As you know, I do business with a number of organisations in retail. Would you like me to sound a few out?'

'It certainly wouldn't hurt.'

'I'll see what I can do.'

They finished the meal. Ivy particularly liked the sticky date pudding and ice cream.

Ross promised Hahn he would get back to her in relation to potential buyers.

One month later, Ross telephoned Hahn.

'I have a potential buyer but they need to clarify what's included in the sale.'

'Everything; the manufacturing in Vietnam, the distribution outlets in London, Melbourne, Sydney, New York and Paris and of course the trade name.'

'Okay, I'll get back to you.'

Another week passed before Ross contacted Hahn again.

'Hahn, the buyer is Zara. They are offering you $10,000,000.'

'Normally, I would negotiate for more, but not in this case. Tell them I accept. What will be your commission?' asked Hahn.

'Hahn, don't be ridiculous. I'm doing this for you, Oogie and Ivy.'

'Thank you. I really appreciate it.'

Once due diligence had been completed, the funds were transferred into Hahn's account.

She invited Ross and Loretta over for dinner to help her celebrate the sale.

'Have you decided what you will do with your newfound wealth?' asked Loretta.

'Hardly newfound, Loretta. Oogie and I were already wealthy.'

'I'm sorry. I didn't mean to be flippant.'

'I have decided on a completely new direction. I am going back to Vietnam, where I'll be establishing an orphanage.'

'That's fantastic! Where in Vietnam?' asked Ross.

'Ho Chi Min City. It will be called *The Home of Tuan*, after our adopted son. I will keep this house and rent it out in case Ivy and I wish to return to Melbourne.'

'When will you be leaving?'

'At the end of this month. I already have a tenant.'

'Well, you seem to have all your ducks in a row, Hahn.'

'I don't understand, Ross. We don't have any ducks.'

'It's a figure of speech. It means everything is coming together.'

'Oh.'

Hahn and Ivy flew to Vietnam on June 1 1995. Hahn rented an apartment in Ho Chi Min City.

Hahn appointed an agent, Sinh, to find a suitable site to build the orphanage. Ho Chi Min City was a densely populated city and therefore vacant land was nearly impossible to find. Sinh found a dilapidated building close to the city centre. Hanh agreed to purchase it, demolish the building, and build a new purpose built structure.

The demolition took only three days with the aid of a large front-end loader.

Hahn selected an architect to design the orphanage. It not only incorporated sleeping quarters and playgrounds, but also a school.

Building began on September 1 and was completed on 28 December.

While construction was taking place, Hahn approached all the existing orphanages to see if they were over populated and if they wished to reduce the number of children in their care. The Home of Tuan began its first day with fifty orphans.

Hahn enjoyed going to the markets twice a week to purchase the groceries for the orphanage. She would take one or two children with her to help carry them back to the orphanage's kitchen.

Hahn was enjoying her new life in Vietnam albeit without the love of her life.

The children under her care were a joy. The school was achieving excellent results.

Vo Minh worked in a factory, which made springs for buses and trucks. It was hot work but it was a job. Years before, he was a member of the Snake Gang, a notorious criminal group which was known for its cruelty.

Vo lived in a communal house close to the factory in Bien Hoa City, about thirty kilometres from Ho Chi Minh City.

He was sitting at the kitchen table eating his evening meal when his good friend Quan came in.

'Hey Vo, guess who's back in town?'

'Who?'

'Hahn Jones. That bitch that wiped out our gang.'

'You're kidding me! The last I heard, she and her bastard husband were living in Australia.'

'Apparently her husband died in some sort of accident.'

'Do you know where the bitch lives?'

'Yeah, I do. She runs an orphanage called Home of Tuan.'

'Tuan, that name sounds familiar.'

'It should do. That was the name of her son we kidnapped.'

'That's right. We gave him back in a suitcase. Thanks for the information, Quan. I might do something with it.'

Hahn was making her bi-weekly visit to the markets. Laman and Linh from the orphanage accompanied her.

She was examining a bunch of carrots when she felt a shooting pain in her back. She felt the pain three times more. She fell to the footpath, bleeding profusely. By the time medical help arrived she had died.

Vo ran through the markets but could not escape the police. He was dragged away to the police station and then transferred to Chi Hoa Prison where he would be held for six month. His trial found him guilty and he was sentenced to death. Vo was executed by firing squad.

EPILOGUE

Ivy was raised in the orphanage until the age of sixteen. As a dual Australian citizen, she was entitled to attend a university in Melbourne.

Ross and Loretta boarded her until she graduated with a degree in graphic arts. She created her own fashion label called HOI, an anagram for Hahn Oogie Ivy.

Within five years she had become a successful businesswoman.

The wealth she had inherited from her mother's estate went to supporting orphanages in Vietnam. She generated her own wealth from HOI.

General Vo Nguyen Giap continued to live in Bangkok for several years until he died of bowel cancer at the age of 62.

Ross and Loretta sold the transport business for $100,000,000. They travelled the world extensively and they also were dedicated philanthropists.

The drug lords of the Golden Triangle were back at full production within two years. Poppies grow fast.

BIBLIOGRAPHY

W   Golden Triangle (Southeast Asia) - Wikipedia

    For Sale: One MiG-29 Fighter Jet, Gently Used

G   australian casualties Vietnam - Google Search

Jim Richmond | The Anzac Portal

Bombing Missions of the Vietnam War

Phuoc Tuy Province | The Anzac Portal

Nui Dat | The Anzac Portal

Distance from Ho Chi Minh City to Núi Đất - 379 km

Impressions: Australians in Vietnam | The Australian War Memorial

9 Squadron | The Anzac Portal

547-2_ANNEX Q_Jack Fenton- A normal day at Nui Dat.pdf

Finding love amidst a war: Vietnam veteran remembers the letter that changed his life - ABC News (Australian Broadcasting Corporation)

Vietnam War soldiers

colinday.co.uk/Vietnam/VnVillage.pdf

014-Kobahiro.pdf

G   surnames vietnamese - Google Search

a   [Survival: An American Family's Odyssey Through Two World Wars BY Willmott, G. S. (Author)] { Paperback } 2014: G. S. Willmott: Amazon.co.

The Tet Offensive | The Anzac Portal

Tet Offensive | The Australian War Memorial

australian casualties Vietnam - Google Search

Jim Richmond | The Anzac Portal

Bombing Missions of the Vietnam War

Phuoc Tuy Province | The Anzac Portal

Nui Dat | The Anzac Portal

Distance from Ho Chi Minh City to Núi Đất - 379 km

Impressions: Australians in Vietnam | The Australian War Memorial

9 Squadron | The Anzac Portal

547-2_ANNEX Q_Jack Fenton- A normal day at Nui Dat.pdf

Finding love amidst a war: Vietnam veteran remembers the letter that changed his life - ABC News (Australian Broadcasting Corporation)

Vietnam War soldiers

colinday.co.uk/Vietnam/VnVillage.pdf

014-Kobahiro.pdf

surnames vietnamese - Google Search

[Survival: An American Family's Odyssey Through Two World Wars BY Willmott, G. S. (Author)] { Paperback } 2014: G. S. Willmott: Amazon.co.

The Tet Offensive | The Anzac Portal

Tet Offensive | The Australian War Memorial

ACKNOWLEDGMENTS

Martin Humphries. My dear friend who preview read the manuscript.

David McQuoid Vietnam War Conscript

Sally Odgers For another great edit

Desma Pacitto Another fantastic cover

First published 2021 by Crabtree Pty Ltd

Caught Between Two Worlds is a work of fiction. Any resemblance to real persons, living or dead, is purely coincidental.

ISBN: 978-0-6451166-0-1 (p/b)
ISBN: 978-0-6451166-1-8 (ebook)

www.ingramcontent.com/pod-product-compliance
Lightning Source LLC
Chambersburg PA
CBHW030517260626
47157CB00005B/1788